To Katie,
Put your head in here.

CONTACT

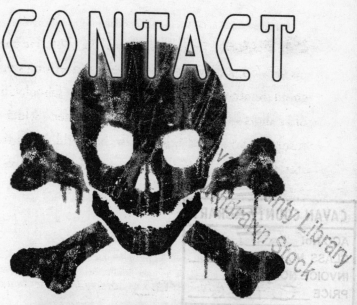

Chris Morphew

THE PHOENIX FILES

■SCHOLASTIC

First published in the UK in 2011 by Scholastic Children's Books
An imprint of Scholastic Ltd
Euston House, 24 Eversholt Street
London, NW1 1DB, UK
Registered office: Westfield Road, Southam, Warwickshire, CV47 0RA
SCHOLASTIC and associated logos are trademarks
and/or registered trademarks of Scholastic Inc.

Text © Chris Morphew, 2010
This edition published by arrangement with
Hardie Grant Egmont Publishers, Australia.
The right of Chris Morphew to be identified as
the author of this work has been asserted by him.

ISBN 978 1407 12462 9

A CIP catalogue record for this book
is available from the British Library.

Printed and bound by CPI Group (UK) Ltd, Croydon, CR0 4YY
Papers used by Scholastic Children's Books are made
from wood grown in sustainable forests.

1 3 5 7 9 10 8 6 4 2

This is a work of fiction. Names, characters, places, incidents
and dialogues are products of the author's imagination or are
used fictitiously. Any resemblance to actual people, living
or dead, events or locales is entirely coincidental.

www.scholastic.co.uk/zone

Chapter 1

**Sunday 17 May
88 days**

Someone's phone was ringing.

Jordan jumped to her feet, shoving her textbook into her bag and whirling around to see where the noise was coming from. Luke scrambled after her.

"Peter! C'mon!"

I chucked the rest of my chips on the ground and leapt up.

"Shh!" said Jordan, like I'd been talking. Her eyes darted back and forth. Then, without warning, she sprinted away across the grass.

She does that sometimes.

I caught up, running a few steps behind her.

A working phone.

How?

I could hardly make out the sound of it over the noise of the park, but Jordan seemed to know exactly where she was going. She sped away, weaving between gardens and hedges and barbeques crowded with people, towards the line of trees at the end of the main street.

Someone had done it.

Someone had found a way past the communications shutdown.

Someone who didn't know or didn't care how dangerous it was to let the whole town hear what they were doing.

More people up ahead. Keith from Dad's office, spreading out a picnic rug with his wife. He shouted something not very polite at me as I ran straight through their picnic.

"Same to you, mate!" I yelled over my shoulder.

I pushed ahead until I was right alongside Jordan. My legs were already burning, still giving me crap from yesterday's bike marathon into the jaws of death.

But I wasn't about to let *her* see that.

Jordan powered forward, unstoppable. She shifted her path, cutting right in front a security guard. He gave us the eye as we bolted past him, and one look at his face told me he could hear the phone too. An instant later, he was running away in the direction of the security centre.

We kept moving, tearing after the sound of the phone.

But the sound of the phone was moving too.

Whoever this was, they'd realized what a scene they were causing.

Why didn't they just switch it off? Why were they running away with the thing still ringing?

Other people were starting to notice that something was up. Some of them pulled out their own mobiles, adding to the confusion, making it even harder to work out who we were meant to be chasing. Others pointed at us as we flashed past, like they thought we were the cause of all this.

"Idiots," I muttered.

We hit the line of trees at the end of the park. The sound was louder now. We were close.

I burst through the trees, almost bowling over Mrs

Burrows and her dog coming along in the opposite direction. I jumped sideways over the leash, nearly stacked it on an empty bike rack on the other side, and ran to catch up with the others.

We'd come out into the little alleyway that runs between the park and the primary school. There was no-one else in sight.

Jordan was racing back towards the town centre, with Luke right behind her. I flew across the concrete, reaching them as they hit the crowded main street.

And then the ringing stopped.

No.

Luke let out a grunt like someone had just stuck a knife in him. Jordan slowed to a stop, chest heaving, sweat trickling down her neck. I pulled up next to her, desperately scanning the street.

On a bench across from us, Ms Benson was fumbling through her handbag. Nearby I saw Mike's dad look over his shoulder and then drop something into a bin. Over at the mall, Neil the butcher was ducking inside with his hand in his pocket.

That phone could've belonged to any of them. Or none of them.

Jordan whipped around, braids spinning out from her head in a black halo. She was still shifting from foot to foot, ready to take off again at a second's notice.

"See anything?" she asked. Luke shook his head.

"Nope." I slumped over, resting my hands on my knees.

Jordan rounded on me. "But you *heard* it, right?"

The question was like a punch in the gut. After everything that had happened at the wall yesterday, she *still* wasn't convinced I was on board with all this end-of-the-world stuff.

As if I didn't have good reasons for doubting it all before. It was ridiculous. All of it. All I did was believe what *should* have been true.

Unfortunately, in Phoenix, what should be true is almost never what *is*.

"Yeah," I said. "I heard it."

Jordan growled and kicked the low wall of one of the garden beds.

"But surely—" Luke looked around to make sure there were no security guards in earshot. "I mean, they haven't put the phones back on, have they?"

"Are you kidding?" I said.

But Luke had already pulled his phone out of his pocket. Two weeks after arriving in Phoenix, he was still carrying it everywhere with him. He hit a number on his speed dial and put the phone to his ear. He held it there for a sec, then sighed and snapped it shut again.

Jordan rested a hand on Luke's shoulder.

"No chance, mate," I said, watching her hand out of the corner of my eye, "even back when the phones *were* working, we never got mobile reception out here. It was only the landlines, and even they were pretty dodgy."

"How do you explain it, then?" Jordan asked, finally letting go of Luke. He pocketed his phone and stared down at the bike path under our feet.

"I can't," I said. "It doesn't make any sense. Who could've—?"

I broke off, seeing Luke bend down to pick something up from the ground. A sheet of paper. Couldn't have been there for more than a couple of minutes, or else the cleaners would've picked it up already.

"What is it?" asked Jordan, looking over his shoulder.

Luke straightened up, wincing slightly at his still-bruised stomach. He flipped the paper over and I caught a flash of red at the top of the page. A fiery bird with its wings curved up into a circle.

"Shackleton letterhead," I said, moving around for a better look.

"It's some kind of list," said Luke slowly, scanning the page. "Like building materials or something. Look: *15-5PH steel plating, bullet-resistant glass...*" He ran his finger down a long line of materials, all spelled out with precise sizes, quantities and measurements.

My eyes dropped to the bottom of the page.

"Page seven," I said.

"Huh?"

"This isn't the whole document. It's page seven." I pointed to the number. "See? The rest of it is probably—"

Jordan cleared her throat loudly. The security guard from the park was coming back up the street towards us. Luke stashed the paper in his pocket and tried to act natural.

Luke acts natural about as well as a penguin in the desert.

I flashed the guard my most winning smile as he closed in on us. He was one of the newer officers. Hadn't been here long enough for me to know his name. He glared back at me, but I guess he didn't suspect us of being anything other than normal no-good teenagers, because he walked past and headed back to the park.

I waited until he was well away from us before I started breathing again.

"So," said Jordan when he'd disappeared completely. "What's page seven of a Co-operative building plan doing in the middle of the main street?"

"Someone must've dropped it," I said.

"Obviously. But who would've...?"

"Someone who was in a hurry," I said, the pieces snapping together in my head. "Like maybe someone who just got sprung with a working phone?"

Luke pulled the paper from his pocket and smoothed it out again. "So the phone..." He stabbed the Phoenix logo with his finger. "You're saying it belongs to one of them?"

I hesitated, not liking where this was going. "Y-yeah. That'd make sense."

Luke looked up at Jordan. She shrugged and nodded. The same horrible, considering-something-that-could-get-us-all-killed look spread across their faces. I cringed, stomping down the urge to tell them both exactly how insane they were.

"You want to try and *find* this person, don't you?"

"We have to," said Luke. "We need to warn everyone about Tabitha, and finding that phone is the closest thing we've got to a plan for doing that."

One day off between suicide missions. Was that really so much to ask?

"Awesome," I said. "Here we go again."

Chapter 2

I happened to run into Jordan on the way to school the next morning. After waiting at the bottom of her street for twenty minutes, I happened to step out in front of her just as she walked around the corner. Funny how these things work out.

"Hey," she said. "Have you seen Luke?"

"Nah, not yet."

Forget Luke. I'd figured out a way to get more info on that list we found yesterday. A way to prove to Jordan that I was on her side.

We walked along behind the school, headed for the back entrance. It would've been faster to jump the fence and cut through the primary school, but I wasn't in any hurry.

"So what do you reckon it is?" I asked, reaching for a topic I knew she'd be interested in.

"What do I reckon *what* is?"

"Tabitha. What's Shackleton's big plan to wipe everybody out?"

Jordan shrugged, but I could tell she'd given it plenty of thought. "Probably a code name for something, right? Some kind of poison, maybe? A password that sets off a bunch of bombs?"

"Alien death ray?" I suggested.

"There's no such thing as aliens," said Jordan.

"No such thing as super-powered homeless people either."

Jordan looked at me like she didn't think the end of the world was something to joke about.

I noticed she'd redone her braids since yesterday. Usually she only did them every couple of weeks, but I guess our death-defying trip out to Phoenix's massive secret prison wall was reason enough for her to—

"*What?*" said Jordan, catching me looking at her.

"Hey, about that list of building stuff," I said. "I

was thinking, why don't I ask my dad about it?"

"No," said Jordan.

"Like, not actually tell him what we found," I said quickly, "just—"

"No," she said again. "Peter, don't you dare."

"But—"

She stopped walking. "*No*, Peter."

Frustration flooded into my voice before I could stop it. "Listen, this thing you guys have against my dad is really getting—"

"No-one's got anything against your dad," Jordan snapped. "We agreed not to tell anyone about this. Calvin and Pryor are just waiting for an excuse to come after us. You really want to risk giving them one?"

"Fine," I said. "Forget it. Just a suggestion."

Jordan didn't answer. She started walking again, hands sliding into her pockets. I followed behind, furious at myself for snapping at her. So much for *that* plan.

Something jolted inside me as we turned in through the school gate. After everything that had happened over the weekend, after seeing what this town was really all about, school felt like a completely different place to the one I'd left on Friday.

I should've known things around here were too good to last.

They'd already started falling apart, even before Tabitha. Friends ditching me for no reason. Dad getting more and more obsessed with his work until I hardly even saw him anymore.

And then Jordan had arrived, and for a while, things were looking up again.

And then Luke showed up.

And then the world was ending.

"Why would your dad know about construction stuff, anyway?" Jordan asked, lowering her voice as we walked past a bunch of Year 8s. "I thought you said his job was writing press releases for the local paper."

"It is," I said, which was as at least *part* of the truth.

Dad was part of the original Shackleton Co-operative team that got Phoenix up and running before the rest of us got here. He'd flown in close to a year ago now – four months before me, and ten or eleven before Jordan and Luke. I'd never been completely clear on why they needed their public relations guy there so far in advance, but up until now, it hadn't really seemed like a big deal.

Jordan pulled a face. "If that's all he does, how would he know anything about…?"

She trailed off, her attention wandering to the other side of the playground. There were about fifty people crowded around the side of the English block, pushing in for a closer look at whoever had been pinned up against the wall. Usually, a scene like this meant a punch-up, but I had a feeling that wasn't what was going on today.

We went over to join the crowd. As we got closer, I could hear people yelling out questions.

"How'd you get out?"

"What did you do to him, anyway?"

"Why didn't you just pull his beard? That's what I would've done!"

We stopped behind some hobbit-sized Year 7s. Luke was standing in the middle of the crowd, looking exasperated. It was his first day back at school since Crazy Bill beat the living crap out of him last week. The school had been buzzing about it ever since. And now the vultures were coming in, looking for a blow-by-blow of the whole thing.

"I already told you," said Luke, gritting his teeth. "I didn't do *anything* to him. He just charged up and started laying into me!"

No idea how to handle a crowd, I thought, shaking my head.

In front of me, the hobbits were whispering to each other.

"I heard Crazy Bill eats human hearts," said one of them, leaning forward for a better look at Luke's bruises. "That's why he was attacking him! He was trying to cut his heart out!"

"No way!" said the other kid. "My dad was there when it happened. He said that guy's girlfriend jumped on Crazy Bill's back and tried to pull him off."

My gut churned and I shoved them both out of the way. "Luke!" I called, pushing my way through the crowd, Jordan behind me. "C'mon."

Luke shot me a grateful smile and started moving towards us.

"Hey, wait! What happened to Crazy Bill?"

"They arrested him, right? Officer Calvin took him to the security centre."

"No, he got out again. My brother saw him escaping on Saturday night!"

"I don't know *where* he is," said Luke, shouting now. "Just get out of my face, will you?"

The bell rang just as he pushed through to Jordan and me.

"What in the *world* is going on out here?" grunted a voice from behind us.

I turned around and came face to face with a balding old ranga who'd just come storming out of the English block.

Mr Hanger. The biggest tool in Phoenix. And in a town plotting the extinction of humanity, that's saying something.

"Peter Weir," he sneered. "Why am I not surprised?"

"It wasn't me, sir!" I said, imagining his head exploding. "I was trying to break it up!"

"It's true, sir," said Luke. "Pete was just trying to get me out of—"

"*Thank* you, Liam," said Hanger, cutting Luke short. "I'm quite capable of asking for your opinion if I want it." He looked out at the rest of crowd, who were still hanging around. "All of you: straight to the hall. The head teacher has called a special assembly."

"Another one?" someone shouted. "What for?"

"Why don't you go over and find out for yourself?" said Hanger, which is Teacher for *I have no idea, but I won't admit I'm not in the loop.*

The crowd broke up and started heading across to the hall.

"Peter," said Hanger, fixing me with his disapproving-teacher face, "the next time I find you causing a disruption like this, I will not hesitate to arrange a detention."

"Yes sir, Mr Hanger," I said, flipping him off with both hands as he turned away.

"Seriously," said Luke. "That guy has issues."

"Whatever," I shrugged. "C'mon, Liam. Assembly."

The hall was half-full by the time we got inside.

"What do you think this is about?" asked Luke as we headed downstairs between the rows of red seats. "Can't have anything to do with us, can it?"

"Don't see how," said Jordan. "Not after Reeve bailed us out. They still don't know we know anything."

We slipped into a row of seats and edged our way across to the far end.

"Does that matter, though?" said Luke. "Calvin obviously still suspects us. And something tells me he's not the innocent-until-proven-guilty type."

"He had his chance," I said, sitting down next to Jordan. "If he and Pryor wanted to do anything to us, they would have done it back in that interrogation room, not out here in front of the whole school."

"Unless they've decided to make an example of us."

"Nah mate, Calvin's been ordered to keep it under wraps. Remember what Shackleton said in Crazy Bill's recording? Until Tabitha wipes out *everyone* on the outside, he wants us all to believe that Phoenix is just an … ordinary…"

Jordan and Luke were both staring at me.

What? What did I do now?

"Mr Shackleton?" said Jordan. "He was the other voice in that recording?"

"Y-yeah…"

"You *knew* he was involved in all this?" she hissed, obviously having a hard time keeping her voice down. "Way back then, you knew? And you didn't tell us?"

18

Oops.

"No! I thought—" I said, scrambling for the rest of the words. "I mean, yeah, it sounded like him, but I didn't know – that was before—"

"Before you believed any of this was actually happening," Luke finished.

"Right!" I said, nodding at Jordan. "Exactly. I never meant to—"

"Don't worry about it," said Luke. "It doesn't make any difference now, anyway. We already figured out he was part of it."

Jordan opened her mouth, probably to say that it definitely *did* make a difference, but then she saw the expression on Luke's face and decided to drop it.

I sighed and turned my eyes down to the front of the hall. This morning was really not going my way.

There was still no-one on the stage. The few times that Pryor actually bothered to show up for an assembly, she always waited until everyone was sitting down before she came out to talk to us. She liked to make an entrance.

I turned back to Jordan. "How's your mum?"

"She's fine."

"And the baby? Is everything—?"

"Yeah, everything's fine."

"OK, great," I said. "That's good."

Oh, yeah. We were totally connecting.

I never thought Pryor arriving could make my life *less* awkward, but I was almost relieved when she finally appeared on the stage.

She walked out from behind a curtain, footsteps booming out into the hall. The whole place fell silent. She crossed to the lectern at the front of the stage, her giant mole casting a shadow across her chin under the glow of the stage lights. Like sunset over Uluru.

There was a loud creaking sound as she adjusted the microphone in front of her.

"Good morning, everyone," she said, smiling up at us. "Thank you for joining me here on such short notice. I have an announcement to share with you all regarding an important change in school policy."

"Great," I said under my breath. The last *important change* had been bringing in that bloody curfew. And the way things had been going for us lately, this latest announcement would probably be just as painful.

The next words out of Pryor's mouth turned that *probably* into a *definitely*.

"Jordan Burke, Luke Hunter, and Peter Weir," she said, stretching a hand out towards us. "Would you three please join me on stage?"

Chapter 3

**Monday 18 May
87 days**

Two hundred faces turned to stare at us.

Stay calm, I ordered myself. *Don't do anything stupid.*

She wouldn't do anything to us. Not here. Not in front of everyone.

I glanced sideways at the others. Luke looked stunned. Jordan was already getting up, nudging him to move. I stood up and started making my way along the row, shuffling awkwardly over other people's knees and feet.

Pryor stared up at us, hands gripping the sides of her lectern a bit too eagerly. I watched her face, looking for some clue about how this was going to play out, but she wasn't giving anything away. Her usual fake smile was pasted across her face.

I stopped at the end of the row.

I could take her, I thought wildly.

She was by herself. Unarmed. If we had to, the three of us could take her out right there on the stage.

And then what, idiot?

As much as I hated to admit it, Pryor wasn't a moron. If she was coming after us, she would've already planned for an escape attempt. There'd be half a dozen security officers waiting outside, ready to grab us if we tried to do a runner.

"Hurry up," Jordan whispered, poking me in the back, and I headed down the stairs to the stage.

The hall was silent. Waiting.

Not that anyone knew what was really going on in this place, but the vibe between us and Pryor was pretty hard to miss. They could tell something was up.

And if they liked hearing about Luke's beating, I had a feeling they would *love* whatever was coming up next.

I could hear Jordan breathing behind me. Steady.

Not letting the pressure get to her.

Keep smiling, I thought. *Just keep—*

A sharp crack of noise from the stage broke the silence. It caught me off guard, and I almost face-planted into the bottom step. I looked up at Pryor, my mouth dropping open a bit.

She was *clapping*.

Some kids started joining in, and by the time we got up onto the stage, the whole school was applauding us. Applauding with no idea why, but hey, that's what you do at school.

Up the back of the hall, Cathryn, Tank and Mike – the people who *used* to be my best mates in this place – were on their feet, giving us an extremely sarcastic standing ovation. I mouthed a few choice obscenities at them and walked the last few steps to the middle of the stage. I'd never realized how massive this place was until I was standing at the bottom of it.

"Thank you," said Pryor, and the clapping died down.

She waited, letting the silence drag, giving us time to get good and freaked out.

I kept grinning out at the audience, trying to play

up the class clown bit. Classic Peter, busted by the principal again. Nothing to see here, folks.

Jordan's face was blank, but I could hear the tap-tap-tap of twitchy fingers drumming against her leg. She was focused, calculating, getting ready to deal with whatever Pryor was about to throw at us.

Luke was a deer in the headlights.

"As you all know," said Pryor, finally getting on with it, "Phoenix High School is an institution which prides itself on a well-established culture of openness, honesty, and mutual respect among staff and students."

Yeah, I thought, *and we also fly to school using our magic jetpacks.*

"These are values that we cherish," Pryor continued. "And today we take those values one step further. I am excited to announce a brand-new programme that will revolutionize communication between myself and the students of Phoenix High."

She waved a hand at Jordan, Luke and me. "It is with great pleasure that I present your new staff-student liaison officers!"

Jordan's fingers stopped drumming.

Applause filled the hall again. Pryor beamed,

clapping like we'd just discovered a cure for cancer.

Staff-student *what?* What was that supposed to mean?

"From now on," said Pryor, killing the applause, "if you have any suggestions for improving the way we do things here at Phoenix High, any issues that you would like to raise, any – dare I say it – *complaints* that you would like make," she waved her hand at us again, "you may address them to one of these three students."

"Wh—?" I began, but Jordan kicked me in the ankle before I could get the words out.

"Don't be an idiot," she whispered.

"Starting this week, Jordan, Luke and Peter will be attending regular meetings in my office to discuss the matters you bring to their attention," Pryor continued. "They will also be engaged in a host of other activities designed to improve the experience of all students here at Phoenix High."

Pryor turned back to us.

"Congratulations!" she said, kicking off yet another round of applause. She stepped away from the lectern, reaching out to shake our hands. "I'm sure we're going to *love* working together."

"She's insane," I said, as we headed back across the grass to the science block. "If she thinks I'm actually going to go along with this—"

"Of course you are," said Jordan impatiently. "We're all going along with it. What choice do we have?"

I didn't answer. She was right, but it still felt good to complain about it.

"We should've known something like this was coming," said Luke. "Calvin told us he and Pryor were going to find us something 'constructive' to do with our time."

"They're trying to distract us," Jordan agreed. "Keep us busy."

"Yeah, makes sense," I admitted. "Can't go off saving the world if we're stuck in Pryor's office. Plus, it gives her the perfect excuse to keep an eye on ... what's the matter?"

Jordan was squeezing her eyes shut, hands at her temples. "Nothing," she said. "Just a headache."

"Anything I can do?" I asked. "You want some water?"

She gave me a weird look and kept walking.

By the time we got to our science room, everyone was pulling out their laptops to write up the prac we'd done last lesson. Jordan mumbled a quick apology to Ms Benson, and we went up the back to our usual bench.

Cat, Tank and Mike were at the bench in front, laptops open.

"Mike," I heard Tank whisper as I walked past, "how do you spell 'polypeptide'?"

"Use the spell check, idiot," said Mike, shaking his head.

Tank laughed. "Oh, yeah."

I couldn't help smirking at them as I reached for my laptop. Tank was stupidity in its purest form. He was kind of like a caveman that Mike and I were training up to fit into modern society.

Or had been, until they'd all decided to drop me from the group.

"Hey, man," said Mike, spinning around on his stool, a massive grin on his face. He stuck both his thumbs up at me and said, "Congratulations on the big promotion!"

"Get stuffed," I said, already wishing we'd sat somewhere else. "You think I asked for this?"

"Didn't hear you saying no," he said. Tank started laughing next to him.

"Right," I said, "because I definitely want to be spending *more* time in Pryor's office."

I waited for Cat to chime in, but she was staring determinedly at her screen.

Oh, right, I thought, wrenching my laptop open violently. *Just ignore me and maybe I'll go away.*

Like it was my fault things had gotten weird between us.

"Listen," said Mike, still grinning like an idiot, "I've got some suggestions for you to give Pryor the next time you see her. How about—?"

"How about you shut up?" I said, almost knocking my stool over as I dived across the table towards him, my rage suddenly boiling over.

Mike held his hands up in front of him. "Whoa, settle down, Pete. I was only—"

"Is there a problem, gentlemen?" said Benson, looking up from across the room.

"No, miss!" I said, dropping back down onto my seat.

Mike turned back to his work, mumbling

something about *anger issues*. I spent the rest of the morning resisting the temptation to punch him in the back of the head.

As soon as we got out to recess, Jordan, Luke and I were mobbed by a bunch of Year 7s.

"Hey, you guys are the … the staff-student things, right?" said a freckle-faced girl I sort of recognized.

"Uh-huh," said Luke.

"We have some ideas for you," said one of the hobbits from this morning, flipping to a list in the back of his homework diary.

"Yeah," said Freckles. "We think it's slack how the Year 8s always come in and steal all the handball courts."

"Their teachers always let them out early!" said another girl. Jenny or something. "It's so unfair! There should be reserved handball courts just for Year 7s."

I closed my eyes. "Are you serious?"

"Of course we are," said Freckles.

"OK, whatever," I said, walking away.

"Hang on, there's more!" said the hobbit, waving the diary at us. "We reckon—"

"Why don't we take one thing at a time?" said

Jordan, with much more patience than they deserved.

"Oh," said Freckles, looking disappointed. "Um, OK."

"Thanks," said the hobbit. They backed away, whispering to each other.

But it didn't last long. For the rest of the day, it seemed like everywhere I turned there was either an idiot Year 7 asking if we could put Coke in the bubblers or a drop-kick Year 12 coming out with a comedic gem like, "I have a suggestion: Pryor sucks!"

By the end of the day, I was nearly ready to strangle someone. Jordan and Luke had started out calm about the whole thing, but I reckon they were both pretty close to losing it too.

"It'll get better," said Jordan, as we walked out past the front office. "It's only the first day. People will get over it and leave us alone again."

"They'd better," I said. "Because, I swear, the next person…"

"Excuse me," called a voice from behind us.

"*What?*" I growled, spun around, then jumped back. "Oh. Uh, I mean, what can I do for you, miss?"

It was Mrs Stapleton, the deputy head.

"I'm glad I caught you three before you slipped out," she said, ignoring the fact that I'd just shouted in her face. She's good like that. "I have a message for you."

"Oh," I said. "Right. What is it, miss?"

"Your first meeting with Ms Pryor has been scheduled for tomorrow morning." Staples paused, fixing me with an expression I couldn't figure out. "She said to assure you she will do *whatever* is necessary to ensure a secure future for this town and its students. She trusts you will agree to co-operate."

Chapter 4

**Tuesday 19 May
86 days**

I opened the cereal box one-handed and started shaking cornflakes into a bowl without looking, eyes focused on the book in my other hand.

"*Utopia?*" said Mum, glancing at the cover as she walked past. "Don't you have a class novel you're supposed to be reading?"

"Yeah, kind of," I said.

"And you're reading that instead because...?"

"Because studying a book in class is a sure-fire way to take all the fun out of reading it," I said, flipping the page with my thumb.

"Funny," Mum pulled some toast out of the toaster.

"My kids don't seem to mind."

"That's because your class novel is *The Very Hungry Caterpillar*," I said. "Trust me, if there was a felt-board version of *our* book, I'd be all over it."

I looked down and realized my cereal bowl was overflowing. I scraped the spilled cornflakes up from the bench with my hand and dumped them back in the box.

"Morning," said Dad, doing up his tie as he walked into the kitchen. Mum kissed him for much longer than was strictly necessary and stuck a piece of toast in his mouth. I made a gagging noise and reached for the milk. My parents have been together twenty years and they're still completely gross with each other.

"So," said Dad through a bite of toast, "what are we arguing about this morning?"

"The usual," I said, going back to my book. "*Peter has a great deal of potential, but he needs to start applying himself in class.*"

Dad started to laugh, but choked it down into a cough as Mum turned around again. Truth is, he was just as bad as me in high school.

"Don't encourage him," said Mum, her highly trained kindergarten-teacher eyes not missing a thing. "You going to be home for dinner tonight?"

"I'll try to be," said Dad, straightening his tie. He glanced at me, then back at Mum. "There was an incident in the park on Sunday that I need to write up for the *Herald* –"

I coughed up a mouthful of cereal.

"– and Mr Shackleton has just brought forward the deadline on this project they've got me working on, so I might have to stay back a bit."

"What's the project?" I asked, recovering the use of my lungs.

"Just some paperwork," he said automatically. "It's nothing, really. Guess I'd better get to it, though. See you guys tonight." He bit down on his toast again and left the kitchen, clapping me around the shoulder on his way past.

"I should get moving, too," said Mum, picking up her basket full of teacher stuff. "Have fun at school. Hope your meeting with Ms Pryor goes well."

"Yeah, awesome," I said.

Mum sighed and put her arm around me. "At least

promise that you won't get *me* called in for a meeting with her."

"I'll see what I can do," I said.

I hadn't told Mum or Dad about the liaison thing, but Phoenix High and Phoenix Primary are technically two halves of the same school, so Mum had read about it in a staff bulletin or something and come home all excited.

"All right," she said, "see you tonight."

She headed for the door, leaving me alone in the house.

I sat there in the quiet, finishing my cereal. I tried to get through the last few pages of my book, but my mind kept spinning off in other directions.

Paperwork, my arse.

Whatever this project of Dad's was, he didn't want to talk about it. Or he wasn't allowed to talk about it.

This wasn't the first time Dad had been tight-lipped about work. A big part of his job was writing up Shackleton Co-operative press releases for the *Phoenix Herald*. He was bound to brush up against sensitive information from time to time.

All of which had seemed perfectly reasonable until

three days ago, when I realized just how sensitive that *sensitive information* might be.

Like this latest write-up for the paper. It *had* to be about the phone.

Whether Dad knew it or not, he was helping Shackleton cover it up.

I thought of Jordan, shooting down my suggestion to ask Dad about that list. She didn't trust him. Neither did Luke.

Maybe they're right not to…

No. There was no way. I might not know everything about what he did at work all day, but I still knew *him*. He was stuck here, just like the rest of us.

So why did I need to defend him to Jordan and Luke?

Because they don't know him, I told myself. *They'd just start jumping to conclusions.*

I dropped my spoon into the empty bowl and got up from the table.

"Bloody quiet house," I muttered.

I'm not a fan of silence. Way too easy to start over-thinking things.

I grabbed my backpack and went outside, flipping to the last page of *Utopia* as I walked out the door.

"Wha—?"

Someone had taken a black marker and scribbled out the last paragraph of the book.

In the meanwhile, though it must be confessed that he is both a very learned man and a person who has obtained a great knowledge of the world, I cannot perfectly agree to everything he has related. However, there are many things in the commonwealth of Utopia that I rather wish, than hope, to see followed in our governments.

I held the page up to the light, trying to make out the words. No good.

Lamest vandalism ever, I thought, shoving the book into my bag. *At least tear out a few pages or something.*

Waiting out on the front lawn was the first piece of good news in two days. My bike was back. Reeve must have dropped it off during the night.

Good on him. Nice to know there was at least one security guard in Phoenix who wasn't completely in Shackleton's pocket. Even if he *had* made us promise never to speak to him again.

Five minutes later, I walked into the front office at school and found Jordan and Luke waiting there.

"Seen Pryor yet?" I asked, sitting down next to Jordan.

She shook her head. Tapped her foot on the carpet. Then, like the question was bursting out of her, she said, "You ever heard of someone called Remi Vattel?"

"Don't think so," I said, raising an eyebrow. "Why?"

"Because," Jordan whispered, glancing up at Rhonda the office lady, "That's who the Shackleton Co-operative bought Phoenix from. Well, the land for it, anyway."

"Huh? Where'd you find that out?"

"The *Time* magazine from the warehouse," Jordan said. "In the article about Shackleton. It says the land for Phoenix was 'acquired from the estate of Dr Remi Vattel' a few years back, by Shackleton and 'eight wealthy business associates'. Whoever they are."

"It's probably crap," I said. "Shackleton and his mates aren't gonna give anything away in an article they wrote themselves, are they?"

"Not on purpose," said Jordan. "But, still, it's worth—"

"Good morning!" called a singsong voice from

39

down the hall. Pryor waltzed into the room, smiling her ridiculous Cheshire Cat smile, and I felt a chill that was way beyond your normal meet-the-head creeps.

"Good morning, Ms Pryor," we parroted back.

"I really am very excited about this new endeavour of ours," said Pryor, looming over us. "I am certain we're going to accomplish great things together."

"Me too, miss!" I said, jumping to my feet.

Two could play at the fake-enthusiasm game.

But then Pryor held up a hand. "No, don't all of you get up at once," she said. "I think it's best if I speak to you one at a time today. It will give me an opportunity to get to know each of you a little better."

Divide and conquer. OK.

That was going to make life a little bit more interesting.

"Who would like to go first?" Pryor asked.

"You want to?" I said, turning to Luke. He was looking kind of nervous. It would be good for him to go first and get it over with. And if that meant leaving Jordan and me back here to spend some quality time together ... well, I guess I was OK with that too.

"I'll go," smiled Jordan, standing up.

"Excellent!" said Pryor. "Right this way."

Luke smirked at me like he knew exactly what I'd been thinking.

"Can't blame a guy for trying," I said, watching Jordan disappear down the hall.

"You can if he's already tried about a hundred times," said Luke.

Like you'd know, I thought.

But instead I said, "Points for persistence though, right? Besides, hundred and first time's a charm, I reckon."

"Uh-huh," said Luke. "So, anyway, my mum emailed Ketterley yesterday to book me a flight home to see Dad."

"And?"

"He said there were no flights available right now, but he'd add my name to the queue and let us know as soon as something opened up."

"Yeah, well, no surprises there," I said.

"No," said Luke. He sighed and stared down at his feet.

I knew I should feel sorry for him, but something else was nagging at the back of my brain. I was missing something.

About five minutes later, we heard footsteps in the hall. I looked up, hoping Jordan would be able to give us some clue about what was coming.

But when Pryor came back into the room, she was alone.

"Who's next?" she asked.

Luke shrugged and stood up.

"Lovely," smiled Pryor, leading him away.

More silence. Great.

Surely Pryor hadn't *done* anything to Jordan. If they were trying to keep people from asking questions about Phoenix, the mysterious disappearance of a student would be a pretty stupid move.

They wouldn't do anything. At least not until they knew for sure that we were a threat.

I closed my eyes. This was all so much easier when I could just tell myself none of it was real.

I pulled out *Utopia* again, looking for something to distract me, and had another go at reading the last paragraph through all the scribble.

In the meanwhile, though it must be confessed that he is both a very learned man and a person who has obtained a great knowledge of the world, I cannot perfectly agree to everything he has related. However, there are many things in the commonwealth of Utopia that I rather wish, than hope, to see followed in our governments.

I squinted at the page.

I turned it around.

And I finally realized what had been nagging at me. *You idiot.*

A library book. Scribbled with black marker.

This wasn't some idiot kid's doing. It was *Crazy Bill*. He'd left a clue or a message or something.

I turned the book back up the right way. And then I saw it. Not *all* of the last paragraph had been scratched out.

Some of the letters were still showing.

I scrounged around in the bottom of my bag for a pen, completely forgetting where I was and that I should probably be more careful, and started writing the letters down in order, in the margin of the page.

B ... E ... H ... I ...

But I'd had this book out for weeks.

N ... D ... T ... H ...

If it *was* Bill, when had he done it?

43

E ... W ... I ... N ...

We already knew he'd broken into Jordan and Luke's houses. Had he broken into mine as well?

D ... M ... I ... L ... L ...

I reached the end of the paragraph and checked through the whole thing again to make sure I hadn't missed any letters.

No. That was all of them.

BEHINDTHEWINDMILL

What was that supposed to—?

"I hope that's not a *school* book, Mr Weir," said Pryor, suddenly right above me.

I flinched, almost smacking my head on the wall behind me. "No, miss!" I lied, cramming *Utopia* back into my bag. "One of mine."

Pryor glared down, seeing right through me. But I guess she was more concerned about whatever was waiting for us in her office, because she decided not to pull me up on it.

"Shall we?" she asked.

I followed Pryor down the hall to the big metal door that led into her office. She held her key card up to the sensor, and the door clunked open.

Inside, the office looked the same as always. Pryor had this weird throne-room thing going on – antique furniture and an ancient-looking tapestry on the back wall and a massive red-and-gold rug that looked like it had been stolen from the Gryffindor common room.

The only normal bit of furniture in the room was a flimsy fold-up plastic chair parked in front of Pryor's desk. That was mine, I assumed. Just to make sure I knew my place.

Pryor sat down behind her desk and clicked at something on her laptop.

Recording our conversation again.

"Mr Weir," she said, leaning forward. "How are you?"

"Sorry, miss?"

"How are you?" she said again, as though it was perfectly normal for us to be chatting like this. "Is life treating you well?"

"Um, yeah," I said, caught off guard. "All good, thanks, miss."

"Good."

Pryor reached across her desk and picked up a stack of paper. "I have your first assignment for you," she said.

"My what?"

"Your first task as staff-student liaison officer."

"Oh, right," I said. "What is it, miss?"

She pushed the stack of paper across the table towards me. I scanned the first page.

Phoenix High School Student Satisfaction Questionnaire

"A survey?" I said, flipping through the pages. "Are you serious, miss?"

"Absolutely," smiled Pryor. "What better way to launch this new initiative than by conducting a detailed analysis of the needs of your fellow students?"

I figured that was probably a rhetorical question.

"I have provided each of you with thirty copies of the questionnaire," said Pryor. "I would like you to have them completed by Friday, along with a summary of your findings."

Ninety copies. That was like half the school.

"No worries, miss!" I said, forcing myself to keep a straight face, not wanting to give her the satisfaction of knowing she was getting to me.

"Excellent," said Pryor. "Mr Weir, I hope you're as

excited as I am by all of this. I know the two of us have had our differences in the past, but I believe that this project could be a real turning point for us."

"Yeah, me too, miss," I said, shoving the surveys into my backpack.

"Glad to hear it," said Pryor. The bell rang out in the quad and she got up from her chair to see me out. I followed her to the door, hardly believing I'd got through the meeting without a single mention of what we may or may not have been up to last Saturday.

It was like none of it had ever happened. Which I guess was the point.

The bell stopped ringing, and I froze in the doorway. There was another sound coming from inside the office, so quiet I was surprised I'd even noticed it. A low, muffled buzzing.

Like a mobile phone vibrating around inside a desk drawer.

Pryor's eyes flickered.

"Come on, Mr Weir," she said over the buzzing. "Time to get to class."

She waved me outside and shut the door.

Chapter 5

"A phone?" said Jordan. "You're sure that's what you heard?"

"*Yes,*" I said again. "Unless Pryor's running a secret beekeeping business out of her top drawer."

It was recess, and we were hiding out in an upstairs corridor in the English block, trying to avoid the plague of Year 7s that was still following us everywhere we went. I'd been in classes with Luke all morning, but this was the first chance I'd had to talk to Jordan since leaving Pryor's office.

"Sorry," said Jordan, brushing her braids back out of her face with one hand. "It's just – I mean, if

Pryor's actually got a working phone, then this is… Hold on. Are you saying it was *her* we were chasing on Sunday?"

"Dunno," I said. "Wouldn't have thought she could run that fast, but—"

"So what are we gonna do?" asked Luke impatiently. "How are we going to get in there and get it?"

"Getting *in* isn't the problem," I said, pulling a sandwich out of my bag. "Just wait until our next meeting with—"

"We can't wait that long," Luke cut in. "You know what Pryor's like. She's hardly ever here. It could be days before we see her again."

"That's just it, mate," I said. "Just because we don't *see* Pryor doesn't mean she's not here. It means she's *in her office*. And even if she wasn't, how would you get through the door?"

"We'll find a way," said Luke, a desperate edge creeping into his voice. "Steal her key card or—"

"No, Peter's right," said Jordan. "We need to wait. We need to be smart about this."

"Easy for you to say," Luke muttered, before I even had time to be surprised that Jordan was actually *agreeing* with me for a change. "Your dads aren't stuck on the outside."

"No," said Jordan, "just the rest of my family and everyone else I care about."

Luke closed his eyes. "I didn't mean—"

"I know you didn't," said Jordan. "My point is, we're all on the same side here." I bristled as she reached out to touch him again. "I *know* you want to help your dad. But rushing in there and getting caught isn't going to help anyone."

Luke took a breath.

"All right," he said eventually. "Yeah. You're right."

"The tricky part is gonna be getting Pryor *out* for long enough to grab the phone," I said, leaning out the window to peg my sandwich wrapper at a kid walking past below us. "And making sure she doesn't know it was us who took it."

The bell rang again. Now that I'd filled Jordan in on the phone, my mind was back on BEHINDTHEWINDMILL. I snatched up my bag and headed for the stairs.

"What are you in such a hurry for?" asked Jordan. "Don't you two have a free period?"

"Yeah," I said, "but I need to go look for a book."

I hadn't told her or Luke about Bill's message yet. No point getting them all hyped up until I actually had something useful to tell them.

But there was definitely no windmill in Phoenix. And since Crazy Bill's last two messages had been hidden in library books, I figured that was as good a place as any to start.

"I'd better go too," said Luke. "Need to make sure Peter doesn't get up to any shenanigans with Mrs Lewis."

I kicked him in the shin. He got up, laughing and rubbing his leg, and started following me downstairs.

A second later, I heard Jordan's voice behind me. "Peter, wait."

I stopped walking. "Yeah?"

"Thanks."

I stared at her. This was new.

"No worries," I said. "Could've been any of us that heard the phone. I was just in the right place at the right time."

"No, not just that," said Jordan, "I mean thanks for being with us in this. Thanks for believing that it's all real."

"Hey," I shrugged, "when you're right, you're right."

She smiled and headed back up the stairs.

"See?" I said to Luke as she disappeared.

"See what?"

"Told you. Hundred and first time's a—"

SLAM!

I took one step into the downstairs corridor and heard a locker bang shut.

Cat was standing alone, about ten metres away, looking like we'd just caught her doing something extremely suss. There was something in her hand. A letter, maybe.

But whoever's locker she'd been poking around in, I knew it was nowhere near hers.

I started walking towards her. "Cat, that's... Whose locker is that?"

Cat's hands were shaking. Whatever this was, getting caught was a big deal.

She whipped the paper around behind her back.

Her face went red, then white.

Then she turned and ran away down the corridor.

*

"All right," I sighed, staring down at a kid so pasty I could almost see through him. The kids in his year all called him Ghost. No idea what his real name was. "What is your opinion of the range of lunch options available at the school canteen? Are you extremely satisfied, somewhat satisfied, neither satisfied nor dissatisfied, somewhat dissatisfied, or—?"

"Somewhat dissatisfied," he said. "No, wait. What was the middle one?"

I tried to remind myself that losing it at this kid would be a bad idea. At least until he'd answered all the questions.

By Tuesday afternoon, we'd decided that the best way to fast-track our next meeting with Pryor was by finishing all her stupid surveys. My vote had been for faking the results. As if she was even gonna look at them anyway. But Luke didn't want to risk it. He didn't want to do anything to rock the boat until after we got our hands on that phone.

So, for the last two days, we'd spent every spare

moment chasing people around the playground, trying to ambush them into doing the surveys. At first, it had been easy enough – there are always a few losers who go nuts over this kind of stuff – but after that, I might as well have been offering people free kicks in the face.

Finally, though, we were getting close to the end of them.

Things in the BEHINDTHEWINDMILL department had been just as frustrating. All Mrs Lewis had been able to come up with when I'd gone to the library was *The Wind in the Willows* and a couple of books on Holland.

Dead ends.

What was Crazy Bill trying to tell me? And why *me*, anyway?

I finished up with Ghost and found Luke thanking some Year 8 kid for her help.

"Done!" he said, flipping through the pages as I came up to him. "You?"

"Just about." I clicked my pen and started scribbling down the boxes of one of my blank surveys.

"Hey, you said…"

"Mate, I've got *three* left, and we've already asked everyone. I'll mix 'em in with the others and Pryor won't know the difference."

"Fine, whatever," said Luke irritably. "So did you ever figure out what was up with Cat the other day?"

"Nah," I said, flipping over the page and filling out the other side. "Couldn't get anything out of Mike or Tank. They definitely both know, though, from the looks on their faces when I asked."

"What about Cat?"

"What do you reckon?" I said, bitterness jumping at me out of nowhere. "Good luck getting two words from her about *anything* anymore."

"Weird," said Luke. "She freaks out when we catch her, but then we get to geography and she's right back to pretending we don't exist."

"Pretending *I* don't exist, you mean. Only problem she has with you guys is that you're hanging out with me."

Luke shrugged.

I finished the survey, shoved it into the middle of my pile, and got started on the next one.

"Hang on," said Luke slowly. "You and Cathryn weren't ever…?"

My pen slipped out of my hand.

"What?" I said, catching it before it hit the ground, mind suddenly flashing with images of Cat, of how it'd been back in the beginning, of how things had almost—

"Nah, mate," I said, grabbing hold of my brain again, "you know I'm a one-woman man."

"Actually, right now I think you're technically a *zero*-woman man," said Luke.

"Whatever," I said. "In case you haven't noticed, I'm making some serious headway in that department."

"Uh-huh," said Luke, scanning the quad. "Well, we should probably go see if she's—"

He stopped short, staring out past the admin building. "Peter…"

"Yeah, I see 'em."

Pryor was coming into the school from across the street, talking to a guy in a suit with two black eyes and a bandaged head.

"Who's that?" asked Luke, moving in for a closer look.

"Ben More," I said. "Works in my dad's building."

"Ben? The one who went after Crazy Bill when he tried to break out of the security centre?"

"Definitely *looks* like he's had a run-in with Bill," I said, grabbing the back of Luke's bag in time to stop him disappearing around the side of the admin building. "Hang on."

I poked my head out to see Pryor and Ben going in at the other end. As soon as they were gone, Luke got moving again, creeping along the front of the building.

"Mate," I hissed, two steps behind, "what do you think you're—?"

He stopped about halfway down, climbing up on a bike rack and peering in through the window.

"You really think this is a good idea?" I said, clambering up next to him.

"No," he said. "Shh!"

From where we were standing, we were just high enough to see through the window to the hallway inside. Pryor and Ben were standing outside the head teacher's office.

Ben reached into his chest pocket and pulled out a key card just like Pryor's. He waved it past the sensor and the big metal door swung open.

Pryor glared at the back of his head like, *Excuse me,*

this is MY office, then followed him inside and shut the door.

"Huh," I said. "She didn't like that."

"Why would he have a key to her office?" asked Luke.

"Dunno," I said. "But Ben's one of Shackleton's top guys. He could probably get a key to pretty much anywhere he wanted."

I stared at the closed door.

And the door stayed closed.

"Well," I said after a minute, "that was boring. Let's go see if—"

I bit my tongue as Pryor's door swung open again. Pryor walked out, grumbling and shaking her head.

But where was Ben?

I stretched up on my toes, trying to see into her office through the half-open door. But as far as I could tell, he was nowhere inside.

It was like he'd just disappeared.

CRASH!

I ducked down and leapt off the bike rack. Luke had just lost his footing and stacked it across a row of bikes. He staggered back, trying to find the ground again, his pile of surveys flying out of his hand.

"*Crap,*" I muttered, grabbing the stupid unco by the back of the shirt and pulling him free. He scraped the mess of papers back together and we bolted back to the quad.

"Mr Weir! Mr Hunter!" called a voice from behind us. "May I see you for a moment?"

Pryor was standing at the edge of the quad. She looked pretty cut at first, but by the time we'd backtracked across the asphalt, her face had shifted back into a smile. "May I ask where you two were off to in such a hurry?"

"Just looking for Jordan, miss," I said.

"Yeah," Luke panted. "We wanted to tell her we'd finished our assignment."

He held out the very crumpled stack of papers. Pryor pursed her lips.

"They're a bit of a mess," said Luke nervously, straightening up the pile. "I dropped them. Sorry."

"He got a bit over-excited," I said. "You know how it is when you're filling out surveys."

"Indeed," said Pryor coldly. "Well then, I suggest

59

you begin analyzing your findings. I will meet with the three of you at lunchtime tomorrow to discuss the results."

"Uh, right," I said. "Great. See you then, miss!"

Pryor didn't move.

"Is there something else, miss?"

"Just one more thing," Pryor smiled. "If I ever catch either of you snooping around my office again, I will arrange for your lives to become *extremely* unpleasant. Is that understood?"

Chapter 6

**Friday 22 May
83 days**

"All sorted?" I whispered as Jordan crept into the room and sat down next to me.

"Yeah," she said out of the corner of her mouth. "It's the one just outside the door at the other end of the building."

We were sitting in the front office, waiting for Pryor to show up. Jordan had stopped on the way here to cram one of the bins in the quad full of newspaper – part one of our plan to get Pryor out of her office.

"You OK?" asked Jordan, leaning over to talk to Luke.

"Yeah," he said, snapping around to face her, eyes

open slightly too wide. "Yeah, good. I'm good. Let's do this."

He'd been exploding with nervous energy all day. Not that I could blame him, I guess. By the end of the day, we'd be telling his dad and everyone else about what was really going on in Phoenix – or we'd be even more dead than we already were.

I just hoped he could hold it together in Pryor's office.

"Mr Hunter," said Pryor, suddenly appearing in the doorway. "You first, today."

Luke jumped up like she'd zapped him with a Taser and followed her back down the hall.

Huh. Pryor was tightening the leash again. No more letting us decide who went in to see her first.

I wasn't complaining about her choice, though.

I looked across at Jordan. She was leaning forward, arms resting on her knees, like she was bracing herself for whatever was coming next.

She smelled good today.

"So what do *you* reckon happened to More yesterday?" I asked, leaning in nice and close to whisper in her ear. It's important to be covert in these situations.

"You tell me," said Jordan. "You're the one who saw it. You sure he wasn't just behind the door or something?"

"What would he be doing behind the door?"

"Well, either he was still in there somewhere and you guys just didn't see him," said Jordan, "or there's another way out of Pryor's office that we don't know about."

"Secret trapdoor under the rug?" I suggested.

Jordan smiled back. "Right."

After only a minute or two, Pryor was back.

"Miss Burke," she smiled, after sending Luke outside. "Please come with me."

"Good luck," I whispered as she stood up.

"Yeah, you too."

And just like that, Pryor unknowingly finished handing out the jobs for our little heist. Jordan and Luke on distraction duty. Me in charge of grabbing the phone.

I kicked back in my seat and tried not to think too much about what would happen if we were caught. This was actually surprisingly easy, thanks to all the other stuff that was buzzing around in my brain; trying

63

to figure out where Ben had disappeared to yesterday; wondering where they'd put Crazy Bill and what I was supposed to be doing with his stupid clue; marvelling that I'd just had a whole conversation with Jordan without getting yelled at even once.

Not that the yelling ever really fazes me. I mean, nothing wrong with a passionate relationship, right? But the peaceful moments are nice too.

Before long, I heard the familiar clunk of Pryor's door reopening. I checked the clock on the wall. Lunch was almost over. If this was going to work, we needed to get moving. I got up and crossed the room, meeting Pryor as she reached the doorway.

"Goodness," she said, almost running into me. "Eager to get started, are we, Mr Weir?"

"You know it, miss!" I said, pulling my surveys out of my bag. "I've got some exciting findings for you."

"Excellent." Pryor headed back down the hall. I followed her into the office and she pushed the door shut behind us.

This was it. Any minute now, Jordan and Luke would start unleashing mayhem on the quad.

There was no way to *guarantee* that what we were

planning would get Pryor out of her office, but I was pretty confident. If there's one thing I've learnt in my time at school, it's how to make a scene.

"All right, Mr Weir," said Pryor, sitting down at her oversized desk, "let's see what you've come up with."

I handed her the stack of surveys, along with a hand-scribbled page of "findings" that I'd torn out of the back of my English book.

She scanned the page for about two seconds, then pushed the whole pile aside and said, "Very good."

A flicker of a smile passed across her face. Not the usual, dopey, let's-all-be-best-friends smile. This one was different. She was baiting me.

See these surveys you just spent all week doing for me? I'm not even going to look at them.

Of course, we'd known from the beginning that the whole thing was a joke, but the smug look on her face was still bloody annoying. All the more incentive to make sure our plan worked.

I smiled sweetly back at her and said, "Thanks, miss. What do we get to do next?"

"Mrs Stapleton will contact you shortly with your next assignment," said Pryor. "In the meantime—"

Through the back wall of the office, I heard somebody scream.

Pryor hesitated, hearing it too, but pushed on. "In the meantime, I'd like you to begin speaking to the students in Years 7 and 8 about—"

More screams, some panicked, some excited.

I opened my eyes wider, shooting for *surprised and curious*, trying to figure out how to help get Pryor out of here. Which would seem more innocent: asking Pryor about the noise, or pretending to ignore it?

Pryor's eyes flashed to the door, considering.

Come on, I thought. *You know you want to. Get out there and see what's going on.*

The shouting got louder, and now most of it was the same word.

"Fire!"

"Hey miss," I said, "did that kid just—?"

Pryor got to her feet and stormed around her desk to the door, muttering something about the teacher on duty. I leant forward in my chair, ready to be on my feet as soon as she was gone.

Pryor heaved the door open and stuck her head out.

"Mrs Stapleton!" she shouted. "Would you please get out there and deal with that?"

Crap. We'd forgotten about Staples.

But then the office lady's voice echoed back up the hall. "Sorry, Melinda, she's gone to lunch."

Before Pryor had a chance to respond, I heard footsteps running along the hall from the other end of the building. A little pack of Year 7 girls appeared in Pryor's doorway, led by the freckle-faced kid who'd been pestering us with suggestions.

"Ms Pryor!" said Freckles. "The boys have set a bin on fire! Now they're putting sticks in it and—"

"Who's on duty?" snapped Pryor.

"Mr Larson!" said Freckles. "He was there a minute ago but now we can't find him."

That would be because Luke had him distracted with a very important question about our English homework.

The chaos was sounding louder than ever. There had to be a pretty big crowd by now.

"All right," said Pryor, exasperated. "Show me."
Finally.

But Pryor wasn't finished with me yet. "Mr Weir,"

she said, pushing the door all the way open. "Out."

"Huh?" I said. "Oh. Yes, miss." I got to my feet and trudged past her, out into the hall.

Why hadn't I seen this coming? *Of course* Pryor would want me out of there. How could I have been dumb enough to think she'd leave a student alone in her office?

Another chorus of laughs and shouts rang out from the quad.

"Come on, miss!" said Freckles. "They're just outside!"

"Yes, yes," said Pryor. She stomped away down the hall, the Year 7s hovering around her like flies on a carcass.

I trailed behind for a few steps, then looked back over my shoulder at Pryor's door. It was still swinging shut.

I stopped walking.

Pryor was five metres from the end of the hall.

The door was closing fast. Any second now, I'd hear that dull *clunk*, and it would all be over.

Had to risk it. *Don't look back, Pryor, don't look back, don't look back...*

I leapt back down the hall and jammed my foot in the doorway.

Don't look back, don't look back, don't look back…

Half a second later, I felt the metal door crush into the side of my shoe.

I gritted my teeth against the pain of it.

Don't look back, don't look back, don't look back…

At the end of the hallway, Freckles pushed the glass door open to let Pryor out. Pryor stepped through the door, turned towards the quad, and for a second I was sure she'd spot me out of the corner of her eye.

No! Go! Get out of here!

And then she was gone.

I let out a breath, heaved the door open again, and stepped into her office.

Chapter 7

**Friday 22 May
83 days**

The door clunked shut behind me.

I dashed to the back of Pryor's office. Dived behind her desk. Stopped and listened.

Still plenty of noise outside, but I knew it wouldn't take Pryor long to put a stop to that.

I looked under the desk.

There was a single, heavy-looking drawer on the right-hand side. I was about to pull it open when I noticed Pryor's computer screen.

Her recording programme was still running.

I grabbed the mouse, hit pause, and deleted the last thirty seconds of audio.

"*What* is going on here?" Pryor's voice exploded behind me and I nearly hit the roof.

But it was coming from outside, blasting over the mayhem in the quad.

Stop. Breathe.

I stared back down at the drawer. Grabbed the handle. And pulled.

The drawer didn't budge.

I glanced up at the metal door, panic rising in my stomach. The noise outside was disappearing fast.

I pulled at the drawer again. Nothing. It was locked.

And then the panic turned to rage and I started wrenching at the handle as hard as I could, rattling the drawer up and down, clunking and smashing and not even thinking about all the noise I was making, ready to tear the whole desk apart if I had to.

Still nothing.

I swore, kicked the leg of the desk, and then swore again as pain shot through my foot.

Then I realized I couldn't hear Pryor's shouting anymore. I stepped back, fists clenched in my hair, staring furiously at that *stupid bloody drawer*.

And then the drawer rolled open.

It just unlocked all by itself and slid out from the desk, like someone was working it with a remote control. And there, sitting on top of a stack of white Shackleton Co-operative notepads, was Pryor's phone.

I stared around the office, adrenaline surging, suddenly positive that I was being set up.

What the crap just happened?

The bell rang.

Just grab it! Just grab it and go!

I took the phone, switched it off, and shoved it down into my sock. It was an older model. Would've been top of the line maybe five years ago. There was a weird bulge at the back of it, where the battery pack should be, like someone had modified it.

I slammed the drawer shut again and ran for the door.

I was halfway round Pryor's desk when I remembered that the recording on her laptop was still paused. I leant across and set it going again.

Across the room. Into the hall. Still deserted. Good.

Out in the quad, Pryor was restoring order. The

crowd of students was slowly moving off to their classes, talking and laughing and glancing back over their shoulders at the scene of the crime.

The bin that Jordan had set on fire was still sending up clouds of black smoke and the occasional piece of smouldering newspaper. Even better, a couple of Year 7s were up against the office wall, getting busted by Pryor. Both of them had long, blackened sticks lying at their feet. By the look of things, they'd been using the sticks to pull flaming garbage out of the bin.

Idiots.

Good for us, though. Couldn't have found a better way to shift the blame if we'd tried.

I crept around behind Pryor, searching for the others.

Jordan was at the other end of the quad, waiting in the doorway to the English building.

"Well?" she said as I reached her.

I didn't stop until I was through the door and out of Pryor's sight. I collapsed against the wall, silent for just long enough to make her think I'd failed, and then I winked at her.

"Yeah," I breathed. "I got it."

And the look on her face was totally worth the five years that all that stress had taken off my life.

We headed upstairs, surrounded by a mob of Year 8s still going nuts over the bin. Seriously, you'd think these guys had never seen a fire before.

Luke was waiting for us at the top of the steps. "Did you get it?" he whispered.

"Yeah," I said, walking past him and heading down the corridor.

Luke grabbed me from behind. "Give it to me."

"After English," I said, shrugging him off.

"Forget English," said Luke. "Larson's not going to notice if we're a few minutes—"

"Like I'd care if he did," I said. "We're not doing *anything* until we're out of here."

Luke turned to Jordan for support, but she just shook her head at him. "Your dad will still be there at three o'clock."

She was agreeing with me. Again. This was pretty much the best day ever.

Luke looked almost ready to push us both down and take the phone by force. But then he just huffed at us and slumped off to our English room.

I shrugged at Jordan and we followed him.

Not that I didn't feel for the guy, but getting emotional about this wouldn't help anyone. I hadn't put my arse on the line for that phone just to get caught using it five minutes later.

We walked into English, and I saw Cat up the back, scratching her shoulder. Her usually immaculate make-up was looking kind of thrown on today, like her mind had been on other things.

Cat glanced up when I came in. For a second I thought she was actually about to say something to me. But then she spotted Jordan walking in behind me and her eyes shot straight back down to her work. I ignored her and followed Luke to some empty seats at the other end of the room.

Larson usually gives us something pretty bludgy to do on a Friday afternoon. Today, we were meant to be looking at a bunch of book extracts on our laptops and deciding which ones were dystopias. It might actually have been an OK lesson if I didn't have the bloody telltale phone beating a hole in my leg.

The longer I sat there, the heavier it felt.

This was actually happening. In less than an hour,

we were going to make the call.

We were going to let the outside world know what was really going on in this place. And then, finally, all of it would be someone else's problem.

I barely got anything done all lesson, but that wasn't exactly suspicious behaviour for me. And it was *nothing* compared to Luke. Mr Larson asked him three times if he was feeling OK. Each time, Luke nodded mutely and went on squirming in his seat.

Jordan was the total opposite. She tore through the work, like that would somehow help us get out of here faster. How she could focus on *anything* at a time like this was beyond me.

But when Larson finally told us to start packing up, not even Jordan could contain herself. She leapt up from her chair and shoved her stuff into her bag almost before he'd finished talking.

"Somewhere to be, Jordan?" Larson smiled.

"Uh, no sir," said Jordan, putting her chair up. "Just excited it's the weekend."

As soon as Larson let us out, we sprinted across to the maths block to get our bikes.

Luke's fingers could hardly work his bike chain.

"Where should we—?"

"Jordan's place," I said. "It's closest."

"Sure," shrugged Jordan.

Despite everything, Luke still found time to stop and roll his eyes at me.

We pushed through the crowd to the back gate and raced up to the end of the street, to Jordan's.

"Should be no-one home," said Jordan, unlocking the front door. "Mum was going to pick Georgia up from school and go do the shopping."

Luke latched onto my arm again. "Where is it?"

I checked over my shoulder to make sure the street was still clear, then reached down and pulled out the phone.

Luke had his Dad's number punched in before we'd even walked inside.

"Put it on speaker," I said, as Jordan shut the door behind us.

"Shh!" said Luke, turning away with the phone to his ear. His hands were shaking. He looked sick.

I shut up and waited.

And waited.

Luke pulled the phone away from his ear. Checked

the screen. Put the phone up to his ear again.

"What's happening?" I began. "Is it…?"

"Shh!" said Jordan, giving me a whack. "Just let him do it."

Luke stood listening to the phone for what felt like forever.

Then a tiny beep sounded from the speaker. Luke pulled the phone away to read the screen again. He closed his eyes, whispered, "No, you piece of—" and hammered the number into the phone again.

Not a good sign.

Luke leant against the wall, shaking worse than ever, barely keeping the phone to his ear. Waiting.

Jordan took a step towards him.

The phone beeped again. Luke stared at it.

Then he slumped down against the wall. The phone dropped from his hand.

Crap.

Jordan sat down next to him and rested a hand on his knee.

Why did she always have to *touch* him?

"Luke…" she tried, but Luke didn't even seem to notice she was there.

I bent down and picked up the phone. The error message was still lighting up the screen.

Unauthorized number.

I showed the message to Jordan.

"Should've guessed," she said softly. She looked almost as gutted as Luke.

Now what?

"You can fix it," said Luke, staring up at me, eyes suddenly snapping back into focus.

"What?"

Luke pointed at the phone, desperation across his face. "You can fix it, right? You know about this stuff. You can take it home and make it work."

I turned the phone over in my hands. "Mate, I don't—" I started to say, but then Jordan was looking up at me too. "Sure. Yeah, I'll see what I can do."

I dropped the phone into my pocket. I think we all knew it was a long shot, but…

"Peter!" said Jordan. "The contacts!"

"Huh?" said Luke.

"Oh, crap, yeah," I said, amazed it had taken us so long to get there. I ripped the phone back out of my pocket and started clicking through menus. Pryor was obviously using this thing to call *someone*. Her contact list would give us a pretty good idea of who the authorized numbers were.

"Got it," I said, starting down the list. "*Bruce Calvin*… Um, OK, let's *not* try calling him… *Victoria Galton*…"

"Who?" said Jordan.

"She works at Dad's office," I said. "She's like the boss of the whole Shackleton Building. Apart from Shackleton, I mean. Anyway … *Louisa*—"

I stopped. No way. How was that even possible?

I'd been over to their place about a thousand times. Surely I would have noticed *something*.

"Louisa who?" asked Luke, head snapping up. "I think that's my mum's boss's—"

"Yeah," I said. "*Louisa Hawking*. She's head of the office complex."

"Wait – Hawking?" said Jordan. "*Cathryn's* mum?"

"Uh-huh," I said, moving on before either of them had a chance to react. "*Aaron Ketterley … Robert Montag*…"

This was insane. Aaron? The doctor? These guys were my neighbours. They were *good* people. They couldn't be a part of all this. It didn't make any sense.

Jordan gasped at Montag's name. She looked like she'd just been slapped.

"Mum's doctor," she said. "He's taking care of all the baby stuff. What if—?"

"He won't do anything to the baby," I said, not knowing if it was true, but trying to be encouraging. "They want everyone *inside* Phoenix alive, right?"

"We've got no idea *what* they want!" said Jordan. "They could just as easily decide—"

"Jordan, stop," said Luke. "We'll look after your mum – and the baby. We won't let anything happen to them."

Jordan gave him a weak smile.

Why? Why believe it from him and not me?

I kept going down the list.

"*Benjamin More ... Noah Shackleton.* Well, obviously. *Arthur van Pelt*... He's in charge of Phoenix Mall—"

Then I realized exactly what we were looking at.

The head teacher, the security chief, the office manager, the residential liaison, the head doctor, the mall manager, the top guys from Dad's office…

Everyone in a position of power in Phoenix.

I counted them off in my head. Shackleton plus seven others. Eight if you counted Pryor. The article in Jordan's *Time* magazine said that Noah Shackleton had formed the Co-operative with eight other wealthy business associates.

Those associates were all here in Phoenix. Of course they were. Where else would they go when the outside world was about to be obliterated?

This wasn't just a list of phone contacts. It was a list of the people responsible for everything we'd been through since we got here.

The people responsible for Tabitha.

"Guys," I said, almost dropping the phone, "there's…"

"What?" Jordan demanded. "What's wrong?"

My thumb had just grazed one of the buttons. There was another name on the list.

Brian Weir.

Dad.

Chapter 8

Friday 22 May
83 days

No.

He wouldn't. Not my dad. It was impossible. *No way* was he a part of this. No way. There was another explanation. Of course there was. I just had to figure out—

I hit the wall behind me and realized I'd been backing away from the others.

"What is it?" asked Jordan, standing up. "Is there another name?"

"No," I said. "It's nothing."

Jordan stretched out her hand. "Peter, c'mon, let's see it."

"I said it's nothing."

"All right," said Jordan, stepping closer. "So give me the phone."

I held the phone behind my back. "No, wait, just let me explain, OK?"

"Explain what?" said Jordan. And she dived at me.

"Jordan…" said Luke, getting up too.

I twisted away. Too late.

Jordan pinned me up against the wall and pried the phone out of my hand.

"OK," I said as she let go. "OK, look at it. Just don't—"

"Your dad," said Jordan coldly.

"No," I said, straightening up. "No, that isn't—"

"Look," she said, voice rising, thrusting the phone into Luke's face. "*Look* at it. His dad is—"

"He's not! Don't even – so what if his name's on some stupid list? That doesn't prove anything!"

"It proves he's got one of *these*," said Jordan, waving the phone in front of me.

"So they gave him a phone!" I said. "He works for them, OK? So do both of *your* parents!"

"My parents aren't getting secret phone calls from

Mr Shackleton," said Jordan. "And I thought you said your dad just worked for the local paper. How is that important enough to deserve a phone?"

I opened my mouth to keep arguing.

And then I closed it again. I forced myself to shut up for a second, breathing, trying to pull myself together.

Calm down. Think. Don't yell at her.

"All right," I said after a bit, trying to keep my voice level. "OK, maybe that's not *all* my dad does at work. But, Jordan, I swear—"

"So you admit it now?" snapped Jordan, and I felt the anger flare up again. "You admit you've been keeping stuff about your dad from us?"

Don't yell at her.

"Jordan, no, I never meant to keep *anything* from you guys. That was before I knew—"

"Don't give me that crap again!" Jordan spat. "We went out to that wall a week ago! You've had plenty of time to fill us in on—"

Don't—

"I don't *know*, OK?" I screamed, loudly enough to shut even Jordan up. "I don't know what he does! What did you want me to say? 'Guess what, guys! My

85

dad's plotting genocide! Better go kill him!' I didn't ask for this, OK? I didn't ask for *any* of this!"

"And we did?" said Jordan.

Luke held up his hands. "Peter, listen…"

And Luke's calm bloody peacemaker voice was all it took to set me off completely.

"No, *you* listen! I've done *everything* you guys wanted! I decoded your files! I took you out to meet Crazy Bill! I went out on your suicidal bike ride into the heart of bloody darkness! And who was the one who *got* that phone for you in the first place? Yeah, that's right. You know what? My life was *fine* until you guys got here! I was *happy*. And now you want to string me up for not wanting to think my dad is freaking Hitler? Well, screw you!"

Dead silence.

I ripped the phone out of Jordan's hand and walked out of the house.

I rode home along the backstreets, blood pounding in my head.

Furious at Luke and Jordan. Furious at myself for blowing up at her.

And the worst part was that the longer I turned it all over in my head, the harder it was to convince myself that there was any kind of innocent reason for Dad to be on that list.

But there had to be. There had to be *something*.

I rolled my bike up to the house. Dad's bike was already parked in the rack at the end of our veranda. He must have been working from home this afternoon.

I got to the door and hesitated.

An idea dropped into my head. It was crazy and dangerous and would probably land me in even more crap with Jordan and Luke. But right then I didn't care about any of that.

I eased the door open, careful not to make a sound, and crept into the house.

Dad was in the lounge room. I could hear his fingers clattering on the keys of his laptop.

I crept along the hall to the lounge doorway, sliding Pryor's phone out of my pocket as I went.

I glanced around the corner.

Dad was lying back on the couch, feet up on the coffee table, back to the door.

Would he really be that relaxed if he had so much to hide?

I ducked back into the hall and brought up the contact list again.

Brian Weir.

I dialled the number, put the speaker to my ear just long enough to hear that it was ringing, then slipped the phone back into my pocket, thumb hovering over the *end call* button.

The clattering in the next room stopped.

I stepped out into the doorway. Dad was shifting on the couch, reaching into his pocket. He pulled out a phone identical to Pryor's.

"Melinda," he said casually, sliding the phone open. "What can I do for you?" He stood up, putting his laptop down on the coffee table, and rolled his shoulders back in a silent yawn. "You there, Mel?"

He turned his head, saw me standing in the doorway, and freaked out. "Whoa, Pete—?"

Dad shoved the phone down into his pocket in the most miserable attempt at a cover-up I'd ever seen.

My brain lost power for a second, and all I could do was stare right back at him.

"How was school?" asked Dad, finally breaking the silence.

I ignored the question. "Who were you just talking to?" I asked, hopefully sounding more innocent than him, at least. I arranged my face in an expression of shock – not exactly hard to do right now – and said, "Wait … are the phones back on?"

Dad flinched. "No, mate, I was just—" His eyes darted back and forth like they always do when he's thinking on his feet. "I thought I felt my phone vibrating in my pocket. You know how you sometimes *think* it's buzzing, but really…?"

"Then why did you say 'Melinda'?" I asked.

He narrowed his eyes at me.

And in that moment, the reality of what I was doing hit me like a bowling ball in the face.

Pryor's phone goes missing in the middle of *my* meeting with her, and then *my* dad gets a call from the stolen phone and I just *happen* to be there to bust him?

Was I *trying* to get caught?

Dad's hand drifted down to his pocket. He pulled his phone back out, face fixed with a stony, serious look that he hardly ever gets.

"All right," he said. "Here. See? This is my work phone. Mr Shackleton gave it to me in case anyone needs to contact me with a story for the paper."

How is that important enough to deserve a phone? I heard Jordan shouting in my head. I shoved the thought away.

"But the phones are down," I said. "How are you getting reception?"

Dad tapped the weird bulge at the back of his phone. "Louisa Hawking – you know, your friend Cathryn's mum – she's set up a makeshift network. It's pretty temperamental, though, and it still can't connect to anywhere outside Phoenix. That's why they've asked me to keep it quiet. They don't want people to suddenly hear a phone ringing and get the wrong idea."

He shot me a significant look.

"Wait," I said. "That phone in the park. That was *you?*"

Dad nodded. "No point hiding it from you now, I guess. I was cutting across the park on the way to a meeting and the bloody thing went off in the bottom of my bag. No idea how it got turned off vibrate. I got out of there and shut it up quick as

I could. But I guess it wasn't quick enough, was it? Officer Miller said he saw you and your mates coming after me."

Why was he admitting this? Surely that proved he wasn't one of them.

No, it doesn't. You already caught him with the phone. He hasn't said anything you don't already know.

But that wasn't true either. He'd given something else away, even if he hadn't meant to.

If that phone had been his, then so had that list of building stuff. *That* was his big project. He was helping them build something. He was *helping* them.

I caught myself. I'd been silent for too long. "Huh," I said. "Well, now I'm just disappointed."

"I know you are, Pete, but I'm sure the rest of the phones will be back on before—"

"Not about *that*," I said, forcing a smile. "I'm disappointed that I was outrun by *you*."

"Whoa, hey, come on," said Dad. "I came first place in my uni marathon!"

"Whatever," I said. "Mum told me you won that thing because it rained and only two other people showed up."

"Yeah," said Dad, "and I beat *both* of them."

He was being so normal. For Dad, anyway. And my dad is not what you'd call a complicated man. I couldn't believe that his side of this conversation was just an act.

Why not? Your side of it is.

"Pete, listen," said Dad, sidestepping around the couch towards me, suddenly serious again, "you need to promise me you won't tell anyone about the phones."

"Sure," I said, taking an involuntary step back. "No worries."

"Especially not Luke and Jordan."

"Um, OK," I said.

Had he even met Luke and Jordan before? Why was he so sure they were the ones I'd want to run out and tell?

"I'm serious, Pete. Those two are…"

"What?" I said.

"I'm just not sure it's a smart move for you to keep spending so much time with them." He paused again, like he was choosing his words extremely carefully. "I don't want to see you get into any trouble."

"Right, because I *never* got into any trouble before they got here."

"I mean *real* trouble," said Dad, a weird darkness creeping into his voice. It was like someone had just dumped ice down my back.

"Dad, c'mon, they're not – Jordan and Luke just— They're just curious, you know?"

No! I thought, regretting the words as soon as they were out of my mouth.

Dad took another step towards me. "Curious about what?" he asked.

"Like … I don't know," I said, brain screaming at me not to say anything else stupid. "It's just, you know, they both just got here, and neither of their parents work in the Shackleton Building, so…"

Dad folded his arms and turned his head up to the ceiling, like he was deciding on something.

"Tell you what," he said, suddenly normal again. "I've got to go into the office on Sunday to take care of a couple of things. Why don't I take the three of you in with me? I'll give you the grand tour and prove to your mates that they've got nothing to be *curious* about."

"All right," I said, feeling nauseous. But what else

93

was I meant to say? "Sure."

Dad reached around to clap me on the shoulder. "Great! All set, then. Listen mate, I'd better get back to work."

"Uh-huh. Yeah, I've got some homework I should probably get onto," I lied.

"Good on you," said Dad. He held up his phone again. "Remember," he winked, dropping it into his pocket, "you never saw this."

"Never saw what?" I grinned, heading for the door.

Dad sat back on the couch and reached for his laptop.

I climbed up the stairs to my bedroom, head throbbing, and crashed onto my bed.

I just wanted to sleep. I wanted to go to bed and sleep away the next eighty-three days and if the world ended, at least I wouldn't have to watch my dad help make that happen.

I pulled up the covers and rolled onto my side, staring across the room at the extra bookshelves that Dad put in the week before Mum and I arrived in Phoenix.

Behind the windmill, I thought vaguely.

And suddenly I was kicking the covers off and staggering out of bed and stumbling across to the other side of the room. I stuck both hands into the narrow gap between the bookcase and the wall, and started grabbing at the big wooden frame I'd hidden there.

When Mum and I first got here, I'd come up to my room to find this stupid framed picture of a grassy field hanging on the wall. I wanted to get rid of it, but Mum had said not to throw it out, so I just shoved it down here behind the bookcase.

I clawed the picture back out again and laid it on the carpet.

A grassy field.

A grassy field with a giant freaking windmill standing in the middle of it.

You moron.

How could I have wasted three days on this?

I flipped the frame over and started prying open the little metal tab things holding the picture in place.

Come on, Bill, you bloody maniac, give me something to work with here…

I pulled back the last tab and lifted up the heavy

sheet of cardboard at the back of the frame. And there it was.

A print-out of an email, with six pages of photos underneath.

And if I'd believed that decoding Crazy Bill's clue would make me feel *better* about our chances of surviving this mess ... I was even dumber than I thought.

Chapter 9

Saturday 23 May
82 days

I woke up to the sound of a fist banging against my bedroom door.

Jordan, I thought. *The photos – shouldn't have yelled at her – Dad – Crazy Bill – so much blood – windmill – he wants to take us to the Shackleton Building – Jordan...*

"Peter?" Mum called through the door.

I dragged my head up from the pillow to look at the clock.

10.28 a.m.

What kind of time is that to be out of bed on a Saturday?

"I'm sleeping!" I called back through the door, closing my eyes again.

I heard the door ease open.

"You have visitors," said Mum.

"Wha—?"

"You – have – *friends* – here – to – *see* – you," said Mum, speaking slowly and clearly like I was one of her ESL kids.

"Oh," I murmured, gathering the strength to sit up. "Hang on, just give me a minute to—"

The door swung open and Jordan and Luke walked in.

Jordan. Over at my house for the first time ever. And there I was, half-asleep, hair messed up.

Wearing freaking lightsaber pyjamas.

Awesome. Thanks, Mum.

Fortunately, Jordan looked almost as awkward as I did.

"Hey," I said, sitting up.

"Hey…" she said hesitantly, stepping towards me. "We came – *I* came to apologize for yesterday."

"Where's my dad?" I mumbled.

"Out, I think," said Luke, closing the bedroom

door behind him.

"OK," I said, trying to smooth down my hair. "Good."

"I was out of line, ripping into you like that," Jordan went on. "*Whatever* your dad's story is, you're in this as much as we are. I was just – I guess I was still wound up about the phone not working, and…"

"Don't worry about it," I said. As if I was ever *not* going to accept her apology. "I – you weren't the only one who overreacted."

I got up and moved towards her, pretty sure this was a hug moment.

Jordan turned away and went to pull open my blinds.

OK, maybe not.

Probably just not a hug person.

I sat back down on the edge of my bed, just watching her for a minute. She was wearing her T-shirt with the green hearts – the same one she'd had on the day she arrived in Phoenix.

"I found out some more stuff about the phones," I said, breaking the silence again.

That got a reaction.

"Settle down, it's nothing good," I said. "Turns out they can't call *any* outside numbers. They're running on a short-range network that Co-operative people set up to call each other inside the town."

"How do you know that?" said Luke, clearly not wanting to believe me.

"Because…" I trailed off at the look on Jordan's face. "OK, first you have to promise not to kill me."

Jordan's expression didn't change.

"Just hurry up and tell us," said Luke.

"OK, fine," I said. "Yesterday afternoon, I used Pryor's phone to call my dad."

Fire blazed up behind Jordan's eyes, and I could tell that she badly wanted to blow up at me again.

"Yeah, I know, I know, it was stupid," I said hurriedly. "But it's all right. I didn't let him see our phone and I hung up on him as soon as he answered. He doesn't know it was me that called."

Jordan's shoulders relaxed, but only a bit.

"Here's the other thing, though: he wants to take us to the Shackleton Building tomorrow."

The shoulders arched right back up again. "What for?" she asked. "Your dad doesn't even know us."

I hesitated, *really* not keen to admit that I'd been the one who brought it up.

"Calvin or Pryor or someone probably put him up to it," said Luke.

"Right," I said, latching onto Luke's explanation.

"It's a trap," said Jordan immediately.

My chest heaved.

No. Even if Dad *was* working with Shackleton, he would never go that far. He wouldn't turn me over to them.

"We're *already* trapped," said Luke. "They can grab us anytime they want. This is probably just one more way for them to try and convince us that there's nothing weird going on."

"And it's great for us, right?" I said. "Perfect chance to have a look around in there."

"Definitely," said Luke, getting more animated by the second. "And the Co-operative must have *some* way of communicating with the outside world, right? Even if it's just to make sure no-one else finds out where we are before doomsday."

"That's true," said Jordan slowly.

Oh, right, of course. Now that *Luke* wanted to go,

it was suddenly an awesome idea.

Thankfully, that wasn't all I had up my sleeve.

"I found something else too," I said, dashing over to the bookcase again. I'd put the picture frame back together last night, to make sure Mum or Dad didn't come in and find it. "Check this out."

I dragged the picture out again and pulled back the tabs around the edge. I flipped the cardboard over, lifting it up for the others to see.

Luke made a noise that was somewhere between shouting and choking.

Jordan just stared at me, horrified, like she thought *I'd* made this thing.

"No, Jordan, I—"

"It's an email," said Luke, pointing at the top of the first page.

It was. An email from Mr Shackleton to Victoria Galton, dated nearly two years ago, with the subject line, *Re: Tabitha: Trial 4.05.1 – 4.05.8.*

Tori,
Certainly a step in the right direction!
Keep me posted,

Noah

>*Sir,*

>*Here are the results from the latest trial. Obviously,*
>*there is still much to be done to ensure that we're left*
>*with a viable ecosystem at the end of the project, but*
>*as you can see, we have made some solid progress this*
>*time around.*
>*Victoria*
>

Then came the photos. There were sixteen of them printed out under the text of the email, all grouped into pairs.

Before and after.

The *before* shots each showed a different animal. A rat, a rabbit, a sheep, a horse, a pigeon, a cow, a German shepherd, a chimp. Each one was standing in the middle of a small, grey room that I assumed was part of a laboratory or something.

The *after* shots were barely recognizable. Just bones and blood and hunks of meat.

Whatever was left after Tabitha had finished with them.

"It's like—" Luke said eventually. "They look like…Like they were blown up from the inside, or…"

"There's no skin," said Jordan.

"Yeah," I said. "It's all just … insides. Like their skin's been eaten away or something."

"What could do that?" asked Luke. "Insects? Like, a plague of something?"

"I dunno," I said. "But I've got a feeling we're going to find out."

I pointed to the bottom corner of the frame. At the end of the last page, right under the pile of mess that had once been a chimpanzee, Crazy Bill had taped a rusty silver key. Three words were scribbled next to it in his weird, blocky handwriting:

More to come.

Chapter 10

**Sunday 24 May
81 days**

"So, I was looking at that magazine article again," said Jordan as we left the mall and headed out into the main street. Dad had organized to meet us at two, so we'd decided to grab some lunch on the way in. "I noticed something in one of the photos. The one of Shackleton shaking hands with Dr Montag in the medical centre."

"What about it?" I asked, jumping at the chance to talk about something other than dismembered animal corpses for a while.

"Off to the side, you can see the edge of something metal," said Jordan. "I think it's a door like Pryor's."

"Montag's office?" Luke suggested.

"Don't think so," I said. "Not the one he takes patients into, anyway."

"I didn't see anything like that when I was there," said Luke.

"You *were* unconscious on the way in," Jordan pointed out, dodging as a couple of bikes shot across in front of her. "You're right, though. I haven't seen it either. Then again, it's not like we've been looking for it."

I stuck a hand in my pocket, fingers brushing against Crazy Bill's key. I doubted whether something this old and rusty would open anything in the Shackleton Building, but I'd brought it along just in case.

We started cutting around the fountain, towards the Shackleton Building. I spotted Reeve coming past in the opposite direction. Out on security patrol, despite his injuries.

You'd think having his arm broken and his face smashed in would've qualified him for a bit of time off. But I guess when you're plotting world domination, you want all hands on deck.

"Hey mate," I said as he approached, "thanks for getting our bikes…"

Reeve walked straight past us without even making eye contact.

"Whatever," I said, looking ahead to the Shackleton Building.

Dad was already out the front, waiting.

This is a mistake, I thought suddenly. But I didn't say anything to the others, and we kept on walking, right past our chance to back out.

"Hi guys." Dad reached out to shake hands with Jordan and Luke. He was smiling, but it would've been pretty hard to miss the distrust in his eyes. "I'm Peter's dad. Ready to start the tour?"

"Ready when you are, Mr Weir," said Luke, with slightly too much enthusiasm.

"Right," said Dad, "let's get started, then."

He led us through the black sliding doors, into the welcome centre – a massive gleaming-white, high-ceilinged room that took up half the ground floor.

Jordan's face flashed with surprise. From the outside, I guess this place looked kind of dark and ominous, but the inside was the total opposite. Light streamed in through the tinted windows and, looking back through the one-way glass, you could see straight out into the main street.

Inside, businesspeople hovered around coffee carts. Wall-mounted computer monitors cycled through ads and schedules and town news. A giant indoor waterfall splashed down across the wall on the right.

So far, none of this was new to me. The ground floor was all public-access, and I'd been here plenty of times when I was meeting Dad after work. But everything past this room was a mystery.

"All right, so, here we are in the welcome centre," said Dad, as we reached the back of the room. He put a hand on one of three big sets of double doors spaced along the back wall. "And through here," he said, pushing the door open, "is our town hall."

We peered through the doorway, into a huge, dark room that looked like a giant-sized version of the school hall. I couldn't remember it ever being used before.

"What's it for?" asked Luke as Dad pulled the door shut again.

Dad shrugged. "For whenever we need to get the whole town together in the same place."

Like when Shackleton announces he's just turned the whole outside world into mounds of guts, I thought.

That was definitely going to make for an interesting town meeting.

"C'mon," said Dad, waving us over to the lifts, "I'll show you the rest."

The doors slid open and we piled inside. We were the only ones in the lift, so Dad went over and pushed all the buttons. I watched the doors slide shut again, sealing us in.

"So that's the ground floor," said Dad as the lift jerked upwards. "Next stop: cafeteria."

The doors opened and, sure enough, we found ourselves looking out on a big room lined with tables and chairs, with a long buffet table off to one side.

At the table nearest to us, a few of Dad's mates were getting stuck into big plates of something dark red and meaty that made my stomach turn in on itself. They called Dad over to join them, but he held up a hand and said, "Later."

Apart from that table, the cafeteria was pretty empty. There were a couple of people waiting to use the lift, including Keith, the guy whose picnic I'd run through when we were chasing the phone. He glanced at the lift buttons, then snorted like he was sure I was the one who'd pressed them all.

The lift started moving again.

I leant back against the wall. Jordan seemed disappointed. So far, this was exactly what a trip to your dad's work *should* be: a waste of time.

"Level two is meeting rooms," said Dad, lowering his voice now that there were other people in here with us.

The lift slowed to a stop, opening onto a long, white hallway lined with glass doors.

"See?" said Dad, as Keith and his mate squeezed out and headed down the hall. "Two dozen of them, all the same. I've had meetings in every one, and I can *assure* you, there's nothing in there except tables, chairs and— Ah, hi boys!"

Two more men had walked out through a door to our right. Mr Ketterley and Dr Montag.

And whatever the meat in the cafeteria had done to my stomach, it was nothing compared to seeing these guys coming towards us.

They froze halfway into the lift. Dad clearly hadn't run his tour plans past these two.

"Oh, hey kids," said Ketterley, recovering first and sending a look in Dad's direction. "What brings you here?" He joined us inside, and the doctor followed him.

Dad shrugged. "Pete and his mates have it in their heads that there's something weird going on in the building. Thought I'd bring them in and show them everything's above board."

I think I might have had a small stroke right there and then.

Even if Dad *wasn't* out to get us, he'd get us killed anyway with comments like that.

"No," said Luke hurriedly, "Mr Weir, I think you've misunderstood what we—"

The lift doors slid open again. This time, we were looking at a sprawling open-plan office space. Dozens of suits swarming around desks and whiteboards and computer stations. Bunch of guys I knew. Couldn't see Shackleton doing anything dodgy here. Not with this many people around.

Montag and Ketterley got out.

"Hey doc, we still on for Tuesday?" asked Dad, holding the door.

"Assuming you're ready by then," said Montag. He gave Dad a look, like he didn't think now was the time to talk about it.

"Almost there," said Dad. "Just costing a few of the parts and I'll be good to—"

"Money is no object, Brian," said the doctor. "Just make sure it works."

"Oh, it'll work, doc," Dad grinned, pulling his arm away from the door. "Don't you worry about that."

Montag nodded, and he and Ketterley walked away into the offices. I had just enough time to see Ketterley reaching for something in his pocket before the doors closed again.

Dad smiled to himself.

I couldn't even look at him.

Before Phoenix, Dad used to be a mechanical engineer for this massive construction company. But he'd talked for ages about giving it all up to become a writer, and moving out here to work for the local paper was supposed to be his big career change. Trading in the high-pressure city job to pursue his real passion. That was story he'd fed Mum and me.

But apparently, it was all a load of crap. Apparently,

Dad's real passion was actually designing Shackleton Co-operative death machines.

The lift started moving again and Dad kept talking as though there'd been no interruption to our tour. "We call *that* floor the Hive. It's where they handle all the day-to-day logistical stuff – water, electricity, maintenance, intranet…"

The lift pulled to a stop.

"And *this*," said Dad, stepping out through the opening doors, "is where all the cool kids hang out. Top floor. C'mon, I'll show you my office."

We followed Dad out of the lift, into a waiting room place that was kind of like the front office at school. A woman raised an eyebrow at us from behind a desk.

"Reeve's wife," I murmured. "From the park, remember?"

Dad said hi to her, and then took us away down a long, wide corridor. There were doors along both sides, stencilled with people's names.

"Nice paintings," said Jordan, pointing to one of the frames that hung between the doorways. It was all weird abstract stuff, but most of the pictures looked like they were meant to be animals.

"Yeah," said Dad, "Mr Shackleton did them himself. He's a pretty big environmentalist."

I bit my tongue. It was almost funny. Almost.

I turned to catch Jordan's reaction, and realized that she'd fallen behind. She was leaning against the wall, doubled over with her eyes closed, like someone had punched her in the stomach.

"Whoa, Jordan," I said, running back to help her. "You OK?" I tried to take her by the arm but she shook me off.

"Yeah … fine…" she said, straightening up.

By now, Luke and Dad were both looking back as well.

"What happened?" asked Luke.

"Nothing," said Jordan, "I just thought…" She squeezed her eyes shut, then opened them again. "Never mind. I'm fine."

Dad hesitated for a sec, shooting her a look that might have been concern or suspicion or just curiosity, then kept walking.

We continued down the hall until we came to a door marked *WEIR*. Dad pulled out his keys.

Luke tapped me on the shoulder and pointed to

the opposite wall, to another handle-less steel door, just like Pryor's.

"Hey Dad, what's in there?" I asked, hopefully sounding offhand. "Is that Shackleton's office?"

"No, Mr Shackleton's up there," said Dad, indicating a door at the end of the corridor. "That's just a store cupboard."

"A store cupboard? What have you got in there, solid gold—?"

I stopped talking. The door at the end of the corridor had just swung open.

Mr Shackleton was striding towards us, eyes locked on my dad. Fancy suit, old man hair, face like a cadaver. He'd always creeped me out a bit, even before I knew what a psycho he was.

Officer Calvin was right behind him, limping along on his crutch, but still looking like he could break me in half one-handed. He had an expression of barely contained fury on his face.

An expression that said he might just kill us all here and now and be done with it.

Jordan's eyes flashed between the two men. I realized it was the first time she or Luke had seen Shackleton outside of that magazine article.

Mr Shackleton closed in. At the last second, his attention shifted to me.

"Peter," he said with a warm, grandfatherly smile, "how nice to see you again."

"Thanks," I said, getting myself together enough to reach out and shake his hand. "You too."

"And you must be Jordan Burke," said Shackleton, putting a hand on Jordan's shoulder. She flinched slightly at the touch, but smiled up at him. "Exciting news about your mother's pregnancy! How is she doing?"

My hands were twitching. I tried to keep them still, straining against the sudden, violent impulse to dive over there and rip his arm right out of its socket.

"Fine," said Jordan. "Good. She's good."

"Excellent," Shackleton beamed, releasing his grip.

I shoved my hands into my pockets. If he did *anything* to her, I swore I was going to kill him.

"And here's our newest arrival!" said Shackleton, extending a hand to Luke. "I trust that you and your mother have had no trouble settling in?"

"No, sir," said Luke. "Everything's going great."

"Glad to hear it," said Shackleton, wiping his hand

on the front of his suit. He turned to my dad. "Aaron tells me you've taken it upon yourself to show Peter and his friends around our building."

How did he know?

But the answer was obvious. Ketterley must have phoned ahead.

"Yes, sir," said Dad. "I had a bit of time up my sleeve, so I thought I'd—"

"You're aware that the upper levels of the Shackleton Building are not open to the public," Mr Shackleton cut in. It wasn't a question. He started walking down the corridor, back the way we'd come, waving a hand to indicate that we should follow him.

"Yes, Mr Shackleton," said Dad. "I was only giving them a quick look around. And since they were sticking with me the whole time, I didn't think there'd be any harm…"

"No," Shackleton chuckled. "Of course you didn't."

I could feel Calvin breathing down my neck as I walked, his crutch thumping along on the floor behind me. I sped up, trying to get away from him, but I was stuck behind Luke.

"However, Brian," Mr Shackleton continued,

stopping as we reached the room with the lifts, "as harmless as your intentions may have been, the security restrictions within this building have been put into place for a reason, and are not to be taken lightly."

"Yes sir," said Dad. "I apologize."

Mr Shackleton chuckled again. Then he turned to Reeve's wife. "Katie, would you please see our visitors out? I'd like to have a quick word with Brian before he heads home."

Katie nodded and got up from behind the counter.

"But…" I said.

"I won't keep him long," said Shackleton lightly. He nodded at the three of us. "It's been a pleasure catching up with you all."

He turned away and marched my dad back out of the room, Calvin clunking along right behind him.

When Dad got home a few hours later, he looked more shaken up than I could ever remember seeing him. He limped upstairs to the bathroom, took a long shower, then went straight to bed without talking to anyone.

Chapter 11

**Monday 25 May
80 days**

Dad had left for work by the time I got up the next morning.

The house was weirdly quiet. I wondered whether Mum had left early too. She'd usually have the CD player going in the morning, or at least be humming to herself. But when I got downstairs, she was getting her lunch together in total silence, moving slowly around the kitchen, like she'd forgotten how to do it.

I asked her about Dad, and I thought she was about to start crying.

"He said he was fine," she sighed, clearly not believing it. "Just wanted an early night."

There was hurt in her voice, but more than anything, she sounded confused. I guess Mum thought that she and Dad told each other everything.

"Did something happen at the office yesterday?" she asked.

I hesitated, wanting to tell her, but knowing things would only be worse if I did.

"Dunno," I said. "No, I don't think so."

She came around the bench and gave me a hug.

"I'm sure he's all right," she said, sounding a little stronger. "You know how hard he's been working lately."

"Yeah," I said.

I packed my schoolbag on autopilot and left the house without breakfast.

What had they done to him? And what were *we* supposed to do now?

There'd been no sign of anything useful in the Shackleton Building. And even if there had, there was no way they were letting us back in there again. I'd spent a bit of time tinkering with Pryor's phone last night, trying to take my mind off things, but so far I hadn't come up with anything. And if Crazy

Bill was trying to provide us with any kind of useful information, his mutilated animal photos and key to freaking nowhere were funny ways of showing it.

I rode down the street to the town centre, taking the long way round the Shackleton Building, putting off going to school. I couldn't deal with Pryor today. Or Cat. Or all the stupid bloody liaison-officer crap. The only thing keeping me from ditching school altogether was knowing that Jordan was probably...

I skidded to a stop. Fifty metres up the street, Luke was walking away from the bakery, holding a paper bag and a couple of coffee cups.

Jordan was waiting for him.

He handed her one of the cups and they started wandering across the street, heading for school. I picked up my bike again and followed them, keeping my distance.

This had better not be what I think—

They were walking much slower than they needed to, much closer together, deep in conversation. Luke pulled some pastry thing out of his paper bag and handed it to Jordan.

You've got to be kidding me.

They stopped outside the school. I ducked down behind another garden bed.

Jordan turned to face Luke. They stood there talking like that for a couple of hours – or three minutes, I don't know – too quietly and too far away for me to hear what they were saying.

And then Jordan leant in and kissed him on the cheek.

Which just goes to show that there is no day so bad that someone can't come charging in and obliterate it completely.

"Luke, you know how you and me are mates?" I said.

"Yeah…" said Luke slowly.

We were out behind the gym, dodging the few kids who still hadn't had enough of us after the surveys last week. It was recess, the first chance I'd had to talk to Luke away from Jordan.

"And you know how mates usually don't stab each other in the back by deliberately trampling over the one off-limits thing in their whole friendship?"

Luke took a swig from his water bottle. "I assume you're going somewhere with this."

"Yeah, I am," I said. "What's up with you and Jordan?"

"What do you mean?"

"Don't be an idiot," I said. "I saw you two this morning."

"Oh," said Luke. "No – Peter, that was nothing. She asked *me* to meet *her*."

"Right, of course," I said. "So obviously that meant you had to buy her freakin' pastries."

Luke closed his eyes. "That wasn't – I only did that because I owed her from last time."

I don't know how he thought *that* was going to help his case.

"Are you serious?" I said. "How long—?"

But I knew. Week before last. When Luke had been beat up by Crazy Bill. Jordan was there to see it.

"Peter relax," said Luke. "Seriously. You've got nothing to worry about. We were only – she just wanted to talk to me about something."

"About what?" I demanded.

But then Jordan burst out from around the corner. "There you are," she said, looking frantic.

"What?" said Luke. "What's wrong?"

123

"Nothing," said Jordan. "I just got an email from Mum. She's got a doctor's appointment first thing tomorrow morning."

"OK," I said, not really sure what I was supposed to do with that information.

"I'm going with her," said Jordan, rummaging through her bag.

"What for?" I asked. "I mean, is this just, like, a mother-daughter thing, or…?"

"No," said Jordan. "It's an end-of-the-world thing." She pulled out her *Time* magazine, flipped to the photo inside the medical centre, and pointed to the metal door at the edge of the frame.

"Tomorrow morning, I'm going to find out what's in there."

Chapter 12

**Tuesday 26 May
79 days**

"She's insane," I said under my breath, pretending to write something historical as Mr Ranga walked past.

"Yeah," Luke whispered back. "I think you might have mentioned that already."

In the last twenty-four hours, he and I had been keeping an uneasy truce about the whole Jordan thing. Actually, Luke was still saying he hadn't done anything wrong, so the truce was basically me deciding not to punch him.

I'd actually started to think that we had a decent shot at being mates. I mean, yeah, he was a bit of a dumb-arse sometimes, but this end-of-the-world stuff had kind of forced us together and, hey, I'm open-minded. But there were some lines you didn't cross.

Neither of us had seen Jordan before school this morning. She'd given us strict orders to stay right away from the medical centre. Didn't want to do anything to attract suspicion. But there'd been no sign of her at school either. And Tuesday mornings were double history for Luke and me, so the next time either of us could track Jordan down would be recess.

Assuming she'd even made it out of the medical centre in one piece.

"Shouldn't have let her go," I said.

"*Let* her?" said Luke. "As if you could've stopped her."

"I could've negotiated."

Luke snorted. "This is *Jordan* we're talking about."

"Listen mate, I can be very persuasive when I—"

"Peter," snapped Mr Ranga from across the room, finally realising that neither of us had done any work all lesson. "What's the answer to question seven?"

"Um ... Nazis?" I tried.

"Nazis. That's your answer to the question: *What were some of the staple food sources of allied forces serving in World War II?*"

"Just trying to think outside the box, sir," I said.

A few people laughed, but unfortunately Mr Hanger is not what you'd call a think-outside-the-box kind of guy.

"Would you like me to leave the room, sir?" I asked hopefully.

"Actually," he sneered, "I think a detention would be more appropriate. How does this afternoon work for you?"

Recess was almost over. Still no sign of Jordan.

"This is not good," said Luke, checking the time again.

"You reckon?" I said, seriously re-evaluating my No Punching policy.

We were waiting down near the bike racks outside the maths block. She was meant to meet us here as soon as we all got out of class.

"Maybe she went straight home with her mum," said Luke.

"She would have emailed," I said distractedly, scanning the playground again. "Uh-oh."

"What?"

"Pryor." She was marching across the playground towards us, looking disturbingly happy. Never a good sign.

"Run for it?" asked Luke.

"No."

"But if Jordan's already—"

"*No,*" I said. "Let's see what she wants."

We walked out to meet her.

"Morning, miss!" I said. "Have you got our next assignment for us?"

"Come with me," she said, veering back around toward her office.

We followed her back over the grass to the quad, kids stopping to gawk at us the whole way. Freckles and a few of her midget posse saw us coming and started charging over, probably armed with yet another page of suggestions for us. I glared at them and shook my head. They stopped, disappointed.

"What's this about, miss?" I asked as we headed into the admin building.

No answer.

Pryor stopped in the doorway to Staples' office.

"Mrs Stapleton," she snapped. "I will tolerate *no* interruptions this morning. Is that clear?"

Without waiting for an answer, she swept off down the hall again, swiped her card, and let us into her office.

Luke glanced back over his shoulder. I could see exactly what he was thinking.

Last chance to bolt.

And then it was gone. Pryor reached past us and pulled the door closed.

I sat down in my usual plastic chair and immediately noticed a couple of new additions to the room.

Two shiny black security cameras peered down at us from opposite corners of the ceiling, green lights blinking.

Pryor cleared her throat and sat back in her seat.

"We have your friend Jordan."

The words were like a knife through my chest.

I felt the panic start to show.

No, I ordered myself. *Keep it together.*

"Have her where?" I asked.

I glanced sideways at Luke. He was staring straight back at Pryor, face completely blank. Good boy.

"In the security centre," said Pryor, "where she is currently being questioned by Officer Calvin. I thought it was only fair to make you aware of this before we continued our discussion."

"Questioned about what, miss?" I said. "Has something…?"

"With that in mind," Pryor continued over the top of me, "I wonder if the two of you might be willing to answer a few questions for me."

Play dumb. Play dumb and co-operate.

"Of course, miss," I said. "What do you want to know?"

"Last Friday, a valuable item of property went missing from my office," said Pryor. "I'd like you to tell me where it is."

"I don't know, miss," I said. "Where did you have it last?"

"In my desk drawer, Mr Weir," said Pryor coldly, "shortly before it was *stolen*."

"Miss, you don't think…?"

"It wasn't us, Ms Pryor," said Luke earnestly. "We didn't—"

"Miss Burke has already confessed to her involvement in the theft," Pryor snapped. "She has also implicated yourself and Mr Weir."

I felt the knife twist deeper, shredding my insides. If that was true…

If that was true, then what had he done to her to make her—?

"Ms Pryor, what *is* this thing?" said Luke. "What are you saying we stole?"

Silence from Pryor. For a long moment we eyed each other across the desk.

"I suggest you don't play games with me, Mr Hunter," she said at last.

A tiny light clicked on in my brain.

She was lying. Jordan hadn't told them anything.

I'd had more than enough run-ins with the teachers in this place to realize when one of them was dodging a question. Clearly, Pryor suspected that we'd taken the phone. But right now, that was all it was. A suspicion. Otherwise she would've just come right out and said it.

That's why we were in here.

Now that they had Jordan, Pryor wanted to use her to get a confession out of us. I only hoped Luke wasn't dumb enough to take the bait.

"Mr Weir," said Pryor, suddenly shifting gears, "tell me, how is your father holding up after your excursion on Sunday?"

I didn't answer.

By yesterday afternoon, Dad had been back to his normal happy self. But he was still refusing to talk about our trip to the Shackleton Building, or about what had gone on afterwards. It was like none of it had ever happened.

Except that he still couldn't walk more than a few metres without holding onto something.

"Don't want to talk about it?" asked Pryor. "Well, in any case, I'm sure he's learnt a valuable lesson about the importance of not overstepping one's boundaries."

I grabbed onto the sides of my chair, and it was all that kept from reaching across the desk and punching her stupid face in.

Pryor narrowed her eyes at me. "Tell me where it is," she demanded again.

I gave her a confused smile. "Where *what* is, miss?"

And suddenly, Pryor was on her feet, shouting down at me. "The phone, you idiot boy! The phone that you stole from my desk drawer! Where is it?"

I reeled back. But more shocking than the outburst itself was the unexpected edge to her voice. There was something there I'd never heard before, and it took me a sec to figure out what it was.

Fear. Pryor was *scared.*

I thought of Dad limping home from the Shackleton Building, and wondered if Mr Shackleton might not have the same thing in store for Pryor when he found out she'd lost one of his top-secret phones.

Pryor tensed up a bit, like she realized what she'd let slip. But there was no point backing down now.

"Tell me!" she shrieked, leaning right across the table. "Tell me what you've done with it, or your friend Jordan may find herself—"

"What are you *talking* about?" Luke broke in, tears starting well in his eyes. "We haven't *touched* your phone! Why would we? Phones don't even *work* in this stupid town!"

Silence.

Pryor rested her hands on the table, heaving with rage, studying Luke intently.

He wiped his eyes on the back of his sleeve, breathing hard. Not a bad little performance.

"Disappointing," said Pryor, finally sitting back down in her seat, "I only hope that Ms Burke will be more co-operative."

She reached over to pull a sheet of paper from her printer, and slid it across the table towards us.

"Here is your second assignment," she said coldly. "You are to have it completed by this time next week. I trust that this won't be too much for the two of you to manage?"

Chapter 13

**Tuesday 26 May
79 days**

The next four hours gave me plenty of time to consider every possible meaning of the *two of you.*

Pryor was just screwing with us. Had to be. They couldn't *really* have done anything to Jordan. Not if they wanted us all to keep thinking that everything was normal in this place.

They couldn't have a girl going into the security centre and coming out injured, or not coming out at all. It would raise too many questions.

Unless they're past that, I thought. *Unless whatever they caught Jordan doing was bad enough to make them think hurting her was worth the risk.*

I argued with myself all afternoon. By the time we made it back to the PE change rooms at the end of the day, my head was a mess and I could hardly see straight.

"Hello? Peter?"

"Huh?" I said, slipping back to reality.

"I said *where to first?*" Luke whispered, crouching down to pull on his shoes. "Security centre?"

"And do what? Ask Calvin if we can just pop in for a visit?"

"OK, fine," said Luke. "So, what? Jordan's place?"

"Not much else we can do," I shrugged, spraying deodorant on over my shirt.

"And if she's not there?"

"Then we work something else out," I said, wishing I could just do this by myself.

Ms Jeffery let us out of the gym and we ran to the maths block to get our bikes. It was total gridlock. I pulled my bike loose and charged through the crowd, almost knocking down a couple of morons who were standing around, talking. Seriously, just get your bike and go.

After a few minutes of pushing and shoving and

rolling over toes, I finally hauled my bike clear of the mob. Luke was still fumbling with his bike chain. He kept moving aside to let other people push past.

"Come on!" I shouted. This was no time to be polite.

I was about to ride off without him, when I saw Cat, Tank and Mike skulking off towards the English block.

Where in the world were they going?

"Peter Weir!" shouted a rabid voice from above me. Mr Ranga was leaning out the second-storey window, comb-over flapping in the wind.

Oh, crap. Detention.

"Sorry, sir!" I called up to him. "I'm kind of busy this afternoon. Can we reschedule?"

"Do *not* make this any worse for yourself, Peter," Mr Ranga spat. "Get yourself up here *immediately*!"

I cupped a hand to my ear. "What's that, sir? I can't hear you up there!"

"Peter!" he screamed. "Don't you dare!"

But that was all I heard. Luke had finally pulled his bike free, and the two of us took off towards the back gate.

"I have a feeling you're going to pay for that," said Luke, swerving around a couple of kids on skateboards.

"Whatever," I said. With everything else going on, Mr Ranga wasn't even in my head.

We shot through the school gate at full tilt, sending a bunch of primary kids running for cover.

In two minutes, we were ditching our bikes and running up the path to Jordan's house.

Please be OK. Please.

I leapt onto the veranda and hammered the doorbell.

What if no-one was home? Jordan's parents usually wouldn't finish work until five, but—

I jumped as a shadow appeared behind the door. It was huge, stretching past both sides of the stained glass.

The door opened and suddenly Jordan's enormous, towering, shaven-headed, islander father was looming over us.

He looked absolutely furious.

I almost ran for it. I knew Jordan's dad was a really good guy, but right now he looked terrifying. And I'd seen what he could do when someone threatened his family.

But then he realized who we were, and the rage on his face dropped back a bit.

"Oh," he said. "Hi, boys."

I started breathing again, feeling extremely grateful that I wasn't whoever he'd *thought* might be coming to the door.

"Mr Burke," said Luke, "we were wondering if Jordan—"

"This really isn't a good time, Luke," said Jordan's dad in a voice that made my blood go cold.

"Is she here?" I asked. "We just want to make sure she's—"

"Dad?"

I heard footsteps from inside the house, and Jordan appeared in the doorway. She had goosebumps all up and down her arms, and her skin was radiating heat, like she'd just got out of the shower.

And for a few seconds, I forgot everything that was wrong in Phoenix.

"Hey," she said. "Dad, it's fine, let them in."

Jordan's dad considered us for a minute. The last

time we were over here, Crazy Bill had followed Luke and me up to the house and started spying on us.

Not our fault. But also not the best first impression to make on your future girlfriend's father.

"We won't stay long," said Luke.

"Yeah," I said, "we just need to catch her up on our meeting with Pryor today. You know, staff-student liaison stuff."

Mr Burke looked at Jordan, who was staring up at him, Bambi-eyed.

"All right, all right," he said, sighing like he knew full well she was playing him. "Just take it easy, OK? You've had a rough day."

"Dad, I'm *fine*," said Jordan. She turned to me and Luke. "C'mon."

We followed her down the hall. As we passed the lounge room, I saw Jordan's little sister lying on the floor, surrounded by paper and colouring pencils.

She looked up at us and exploded into a fit of giggles.

Jordan shot Luke a weary look. "Probably planning our wedding," she said. "I swear, she hasn't shut up about you since last time you guys were here."

Stupid kid, I thought, stepping into Jordan's room. *What would she know?*

Jordan shut the door behind us and her tone changed completely.

"Are you guys OK?" she asked.

"Us?" said Luke. "You're the one who—"

"Calvin said you guys admitted to taking the phone," said Jordan.

"Pryor said the same thing about you," I said. "You didn't tell him anything?"

"No," said Jordan. "Did you?"

"Course not," I said.

"OK, good," Jordan breathed.

"What did Calvin do to you?" I asked. "I mean, he didn't hurt you or anything?"

"I'm fine," she said. "In fact…"

Jordan went across to her schoolbag and grabbed her copy of *The Shape of Things to Come*. She flipped it open and pulled out a bookmark or something from between the pages. She held it up in front of us.

"Are you *kidding* me?" I said.

It wasn't a bookmark.

It was a key card.

Chapter 14

**Tuesday 26 May
79 days**

"Told you I'd find out what was behind that door," Jordan grinned.

"Yeah, but…" Luke trailed off. "How did you *get* that?"

"Actually, it wasn't as hard as I thought," said Jordan. "Montag seemed sort of distracted when Mum and I went in to see him. Like he had somewhere else to be."

"The meeting with Ketterley and your dad," said Luke, pulling his eyes away from the key card to look at me. "That was today, right?"

"Think so," I said, really not wanting to get into Dad again.

"Anyway," said Jordan, "Montag let us into his office – as in, his normal office, not the metal door place – and then he clipped all his keys and stuff to the side of his belt."

"The key card too?" I said.

"Yeah, on one of those little clamp things," she said, miming with her finger and thumb. "I waited until Dr Montag went to type something into his computer, and I reached over and unclipped the card from his belt while he and Mum had their backs turned."

"That's it?" said Luke.

"What do you mean, *that's it?*" I said, looking for a reason to snap at him. "What if he'd seen her?"

"He didn't," Jordan shrugged. "I mean, these guys are still only human, right? So, yeah, I stuck the card in my pocket and then asked Dr Montag where the toilet was. I was *planning* to have a quick look in the locked room and get back again before anyone realized something was up."

"But?" said Luke.

"Well, the first part worked," said Jordan, sitting down on her bed. "Actually, Dr Montag said it might

143

be good if I stepped out for a couple of minutes so he could talk to Mum about some personal stuff."

"What kind of stuff?" I asked, sitting down next to her.

"Pregnant women's business," said Jordan pointedly. "You really want me to go into detail?"

"You know what? Why don't you just keep telling us what happened?"

"Right," said Jordan, shuffling away from me a bit, "so it took me a few minutes to find the place from the photo. It was right at the other end of the building, near the room they had Luke in after he got bashed."

"And?" said Luke. "What was in there?"

"Nothing," said Jordan.

"What, so it was just another hospital room or something?" I said.

"No," said Jordan, "it was an *empty room*."

"Are you sure?" said Luke. "Did you … I mean, you went in and had a look around, right?"

"At *what?*" said Jordan, and it was nice to hear her getting stuck into *him* for a change. "Of course I looked, but it wasn't even a proper room. It was just this tiny little cupboard thing with, like, kitchen tiles on the floor."

It didn't make any sense. There had to be *something* in there. Something Jordan had missed. But my survival instinct kicked in before I said this out loud. Telling Jordan she hadn't looked hard enough wouldn't do me any favours.

"What happened then?" I asked instead.

"I started heading back, but this nurse stopped me halfway and asked me what I was doing," said Jordan. "I told her I'd got lost on the way to the toilets. She let me go, and then followed me all the way back up the hall. When we got to the waiting room, she kept going and walked straight out of the building and across the street."

"Huh?" said Luke. "Wait – she went to the security centre?"

Jordan sighed. "Yep."

"To do what?" I said. "Report some suspicious walking?"

"I don't know *what* she told them," said Jordan. "I went straight back to Mum and Dr Montag and hid the key card in my bag. Next thing I know, Calvin's storming in with two other security officers."

"Bet your mum loved that," said Luke.

"Uh-huh," said Jordan. "She went pretty nuts — and that was *before* she knew what was really going on. Because, remember, this isn't the first time Calvin's burst in on one of her doctor's appointments."

"Yeah, she's had kind of a bad run, huh?" I said.

"So Mum starts laying into him about that," Jordan continued, "and then Calvin says one of the nurses has reported some suspicious behaviour and that I need to come with him, and Mum just *lost* it at him. In the end, they needed one of the security officers to stay back and restrain her."

"She OK?" said Luke, jumping in before I had the chance.

"Yeah, they didn't do anything to her. The guard just waited until she calmed down a bit and then sent her home." Jordan pointed at the bedroom door. "She's at her computer now, sending an angry email to Mr Shackleton."

"Awesome," I said. "I'm sure he'll sort the whole thing right out."

"But that's pretty much it," said Jordan. "Calvin hauled me into one of the interrogation rooms and started questioning me."

"You sure you're OK?" I asked, moving closer to her again.

"Yeah," she said. "He was – I mean, between the phone and going to the Shackleton Building and getting caught out in the bush, they're definitely getting suspicious. But they're still kind of stuck, aren't they, because they don't want to give themselves away either. So I just kept my mouth shut and eventually they had to let me go."

"Hang on," said Luke. "How did you get away from there without Calvin finding the key card? Surely he must have gone through your stuff."

"Nope," Jordan grinned. "My schoolbag never made it to the security centre. Calvin was too busy dealing with Mum to even realize it was there. I just left it behind in the doctor's office, and Mum brought it home."

She flipped the key card over in her fingers. "So..." she said. "Who wants to go have a proper look inside Pryor's office?"

I cringed. One of us was going to have to burst her bubble. I decided to let Luke do it.

"Jordan ... we can't," he said. "Pryor's just had security cameras put in."

Her smile disappeared. "OK," she said slowly. "All right, so maybe we can't get into *that* door. But there are others, right? Montag's, Shackleton's…" She stared into space for a minute, then said, "What if they've *all* got one? Everyone on Pryor's contact list."

"Sure, maybe," I said, "but that doesn't really get us anywhere, does it?"

"It does if we can find out what they're for," said Jordan. "I mean, why *those* rooms? There's got to be some connection."

"Officer Reeve might know something," said Luke. "Although he *did* kind of tell us never to speak to him again…"

"Worth a shot, anyway," shrugged Jordan.

"I could see if my dad knows anything." The words were out of my mouth before I could stop them. I braced myself, waiting for Jordan to blow up at the suggestion.

But the explosion never came.

Jordan bit her lip, thought about it for a sec, and then said, "Yeah, OK, why don't you see what you can find out?"

"Huh?" I said. "Seriously?"

"Well, it's not like we have a lot of other options, is it?" she said, as though it was *me* that had a problem with my dad. "Just be careful, OK?"

There was a knock on the door and Jordan's mum poked her head into the room.

"Oh, hi guys," she said. "Jordan, can I talk to you for a minute? I'd like you to read over this email before I send it off."

"Sure," said Jordan, standing up.

"We should probably get going anyway," said Luke.

Jordan's little sister was still colouring in on the lounge room floor as we walked out. She saw us leaving and jumped to her feet.

"Wait!" she said, running into the hall. She had a red piece of paper in her hands, folded in half and taped together. She gave the paper to Luke and said, "Open it."

She ran away, bursting into another giggling fit.

Luke picked off the tape and unfolded the paper. It was a drawing of a girl in a ridiculous frilly dress, surrounded by a big, wonky heart. There was a note scrawled underneath:

you aer a Good boy.
love GeorGia.

"Told you," said Jordan. "She's obsessed."

As Luke and I rode back down the street, it took all my self-control not to reach over and shove him off his bike.

Chapter 15

Wednesday 27 May
78 days

I got up early the next morning to catch Dad before he left for work. I'd tried waiting for him last night, but gave up when he still wasn't back from his meeting with Montag and Ketterley by midnight.

There was no sign of him when I got downstairs. Just Mum sitting on the couch, laminating pictures from *Where is the Green Sheep?*, looking like she'd hardly slept.

"Morning," I said. "Where's Dad?"

Mum shook her head. "Still at work. I got an email from him this morning, saying his meeting turned into an all-nighter and he won't be home until this afternoon."

"Is everything OK?" I asked, trying to block the nerves out of my voice. "I mean, did he say why it was taking so long?"

"He told me not to worry," said Mum, in a voice that told me she was blatantly ignoring this advice. She switched the laminator off and picked her stuff up from the coffee table. "It's just this project they've got him working on. They're really pushing to have it off the ground in the next week."

"But he'll be home this arvo?" I said, crossing to the kitchen to grab some breakfast.

"That's the plan," said Mum wearily. "At least, it was at two o'clock this morning when he sent that email. Honestly, I know he enjoys the work, but these long hours aren't good for him. He's so tired, he can hardly walk straight."

"Yeah," I said, wishing tiredness was the reason for it. "Listen, can you email me at school if you hear anything else from him?"

"Sure," she said. But now she was looking concerned. "He hasn't said anything to you about all this, has he?"

"Nope. Hardly seen him this week."

Mum got up from the couch and came over to give

me a hug. "You OK, Pete? You seem a bit distracted lately."

"I'm *always* distracted," I said, twisting free.

"All right," Mum sighed. "Well, when you *do* feel like talking about it, let me know."

"Nothing to talk about," I said, hating Shackleton all over again for what he was doing to my family. "See you tonight, OK?"

I stuck a muesli bar in my mouth and headed into town.

"Do we have a plan here," I asked as we walked our bikes past the mall that afternoon, "or are we just going to wander up and down the street until we find him?"

"Since when have we had a plan for *any* of this?" said Luke.

I hadn't heard anything more about Dad all day, which I was *hoping* meant that he really would be home this afternoon. But in the meantime, we'd decided to go looking for Officer Reeve and see if we could get anything out of him about the metal doors.

I looked back towards school, double-checking that

Pryor was nowhere around. In theory we were meant to be working on her second assignment right now. Some stupid mapping thing. We had to stand out the front of the school every afternoon and measure traffic congestion.

Thankfully, I'd managed to convince Jordan and Luke to just leave it to me and let me fake the results this time. They were both too busy scheming about security doors to put up much of an argument.

For some reason, Jordan had it in her head that figuring out those doors would help us get a message to the outside world. And she'd come into school this morning *convinced* that talking to Reeve was the way we were going to get that information. Said she had a feeling, and Luke backed her up.

"We should go to Flameburger," said Jordan.

"Why? Did you see him?" I asked.

"No," said Jordan, "but we'll be able to see the whole street from there. Besides, I'm hungry."

I could think of at least five other places that would've given us a heaps better view of the street. But if Jordan was choosing here, then here was fine by me.

"OK, good idea," I said. "What do you want? I'm buying."

I grinned at Luke. He gave me a pitying look, and we went to lock up our bikes.

Flameburger is what you get instead of McDonald's when your town is plotting the apocalypse. The burgers are bigger, but the end of the world is kind of a high price to pay for extra cheese.

I went inside to order while Jordan and Luke picked out a table on the street.

Mike's mum was waiting in the next line over, still wearing her medical centre uniform. I went to say hi and she suddenly became very interested in a menu on the opposite wall.

Weird. What did I ever do to her?

A few minutes later, I was back with the food.

"Wouldn't it be easier to just go find Reeve's house?" Luke was asking.

"Sure, if we want to get a door slammed in our faces," I said, sitting down and handing Jordan a burger.

"Thanks," she said. "Yeah, I don't think he'd be too happy with us if we started visiting him at home. Not

155

fair on his family either. We have to ambush him in town."

She glanced sideways at the empty table next to us, like she could see something we couldn't.

"Ah, yes," I said, "the old *sit around eating burgers and wait for him to come to us* ambush."

She kicked me under the table. "Just keep an eye out."

I shoved some chips into my mouth and looked out across the street. There were plenty of security guys around, but no sign of Reeve. And, really, he could be anywhere. Phoenix is a small town, but it isn't *that* small.

I turned back to the others. Jordan was making a show of looking around, but her eyes kept flickering back to that same empty table.

"What are you looking at?" I asked.

"Nothing," said Jordan, quickly staring off in the other direction.

Luke leant over to Jordan. "Are you sure this is right?" he asked in a low voice. "Maybe you just—"

He stopped mid-sentence and stood up, staring over in the direction of the medical centre.

"D'you see him?" I asked, getting up too. But it wasn't Reeve that Luke was looking at.

A hundred metres away, Dr Montag was coming down the front steps, talking to a woman in a business suit.

Luke's mum.

"Huh," said Jordan. "You didn't say anything about a doctor's appointment."

"I didn't *know* anything about a doctor's appointment," said Luke, taking a few steps towards them. "Although it's not as if she fills me in on everything she…"

He trailed off as the doctor and his mum reached the bottom of the steps. Montag put an arm around her waist, pulled her in close, and kissed her.

From the look on Luke's face, his mum definitely hadn't filled him in on *that*.

The words "poetic" and "justice" floated into my mind, but I pushed them aside as Luke started running towards his mum.

"Whoa," I said, grabbing the back of his shirt. "No, you don't."

"Get off me!" Luke shouted, and I heard something rip as he tried to pull free.

A bunch of other kids stared over at us from their tables.

"Luke, stop," said Jordan. "You can't go over there."

"I can if you let *go*," he grunted.

"And then what are you gonna do?" hissed Jordan. "Attack Montag? Out here in front of everyone? How exactly do you see *that* ending?"

Luke grunted again, but he stopped struggling. He watched, sweat beading on his face, as his mum waved goodbye to the doc, and walked back around to her office.

We let Luke go and he sat back down in his seat. The other kids slowly went back to their conversations, clearly disappointed they hadn't got to witness another public beating.

"We'll deal with Montag," said Jordan, sitting down too when she was sure he wouldn't bolt. "Before this is all over, we'll—"

"It wasn't *him* I was going for," Luke muttered. "It was *her*."

The rest of the afternoon was a write-off.

Looking for Reeve dropped right off the radar. Luke was too busy fuming about his mum, and Jordan was too busy trying to calm Luke down.

The weird thing was that, as furious as he was at Montag, he seemed to be more angry at his mum for seeing some other guy so soon after his parents' divorce. Apparently betrayal wasn't so easy to swallow when Luke was the one on the receiving end.

As far as he was concerned, the fact that this *other guy* happened to be part of Shackleton's genocidal super squad was a minor side issue.

Also, funny how no-one jumped to any conclusions about *Luke's* mum being in cahoots with the Shackleton Co-operative. I guess it's only my parents who are guilty until proven innocent.

I got home to find Dad's bike on the veranda. My brilliant idea of asking him about the security doors was suddenly feeling a whole lot less brilliant.

I let myself into the house, planning to head up to my room for a bit and figure out how to casually bring up the topic of magical mystery doors without sounding suspicious.

Unfortunately, Dad had other plans.

He was sitting at the foot of the stairs, waiting for me, like I was sneaking in at 2 a.m. instead of the middle of the afternoon.

"Crap," I said, seeing the look on his face. "I mean, hi. What's going on?"

"We need to talk," said Dad, standing up. He had a folded sheet of paper in his hands. I was pretty sure it wasn't a wonky heart drawing.

Chapter 16

**Wednesday 27 May
78 days**

"Um, OK, sure," I said, moving to walk past him up the stairs. "Let's talk. Just let me dump my stuff—"

"*Now,* Pete," said Dad, blocking my way.

I actually gasped.

Dad *never* spoke to me like that. He didn't give orders. It just wasn't him.

Who are you?

I stepped back from him.

"All right," I said, dropping my bag on the floor. "What did you want to talk about?"

"Dr Galton sent this out to everyone in the office yesterday morning," said Dad, unfolding the paper in his hands and holding it out to me.

It was a print-out of an email.

Dear staff,

I've been asked to make you aware of three students whom Officer Calvin and his team have identified as possible security risks.

The students' names are Jordan Burke, Luke Hunter, and Peter Weir (see photos attached), and they have already been caught engaging in acts of trespassing, vandalism and theft.

Officer Calvin has requested that any suspicious activity – no matter how seemingly minor – be reported directly to security.

Thank you for your co-operation in this matter.

Regards,

Victoria

At the bottom of the email were three headshots. My Phoenix High photo and old school photos of Jordan and Luke.

This email must have gone out to the medical centre staff too. That explained why the nurse had been so quick to run off and dob Jordan in to security. And why Mike's mum was suddenly giving me the cold shoulder.

They were getting the whole town onto us.

I looked up from the page.

"You want to tell me what all this is about, Pete?" asked Dad.

I scanned the email again, searching for some excuse, some way out of this, but my brain was like sludge.

"I don't know," I said.

"You don't know," Dad repeated. He let out an exasperated sigh and sat back down on the stairs. "Didn't I *tell* you those two friends of yours would get you into trouble?"

"You're saying this is *their* fault?" I said.

"Trespassing?" said Dad. "Theft? I know it hasn't always been smooth sailing for you at school, Pete, but you never—"

"They're making it up!" I said. "We never did any of that stuff!"

"Pete, Officer Calvin is chief of security," said Dad. "He's already got a million things to deal with. Why would he waste his time making up fake security threats from innocent students? What kind of town do you think this is?"

"I don't know, Dad," I spat, frustration getting the better of me. "Why can't you walk in a straight line ever since you got back from Mr Shackleton's office?"

No answer. Dad just locked onto me with a sick expression that made me wish I hadn't asked.

The silence stretched out. I could hear Dad's laptop whirring in the next room.

It was a full minute before he spoke up again.

"I don't want you hanging out with Luke and Jordan anymore."

"C'mon, Dad," I said. "No. You can't tell me who to—"

"I'm serious, Pete," said Dad. "Don't make trouble for yourself. This isn't a path you want to go down."

"And what path is that, exactly?" I asked.

Dad stared at the ground. When he looked up again, he had a pleading look in his eyes that was scarier than anything else I'd seen so far.

"Please, Pete," he whispered. "I just don't want you to get hurt."

He stood up, wincing, but determinedly putting his weight on both feet.

"Dad…" I said. "What did they *do* to you?"

"Nothing," he said forcefully. He took back the email printout, folded it up, and stuck it in his pocket. Then he reached out and put an arm around me. "Just promise me you'll stay out of trouble, OK mate? Keep your head down and don't give Officer Calvin any excuse to suspect you."

"Yeah, all right," I said. "I'll see what I can do."

Dad staggered slightly, legs almost giving out again.

I had a feeling that excuses were the last thing Calvin needed.

Thursday 28 May
77 days

"You couldn't get *anything* out of your dad?" asked Jordan as she, Luke and I pushed our bikes out through the end-of-day bottleneck.

"I told you, he didn't want to talk about it," I said. "I can try again tonight, but I doubt it'll do any good."

I'd told Jordan and Luke about the email Dad showed me, but not about the conversation we'd had after.

We followed the crowd of kids across the street to the mall, keeping a look out for Reeve.

School had been pretty uneventful, apart from Mr Ranga almost rupturing a kidney when I walked into history. He'd shouted at me until his face matched his hair, then informed me that my one after-school detention was now a week of lunchtimes scraping gum off desks – that way he could make sure I didn't run off again.

He'd probably be even more cut tomorrow when I still hadn't shown up to see him.

"What about the phone?" said Luke.

"What about it?" I said, sick of him going on about it.

I had made *some* progress last night. Finally figured out how to connect it to my laptop and get inside the firmware. But changing the security settings was still going to be a major hassle. And even if I did, it's not like we had reception.

But Jordan had to appreciate the effort, surely, and that was a good enough consolation prize to keep me working on it.

I looked up and realized that Jordan was leading

us straight to Flameburger. I was about to point out how spectacularly unsuccessful our last visit had been, when Luke stretched out a hand and said, "Look!"

Officer Reeve had just walked through the sliding doors. He was out of uniform, holding his son's hand with his good arm and balancing a tray of food on the plastered one. He found a table and the two of them sat down.

There was something weird about this scene, but it took me a sec to figure out what it was.

Then I saw it. They were sitting at the exact table that Jordan had been fixated on yesterday.

I whirled around to face her. "How did you know?"

"Know what?" said Jordan.

"C'mon," said Luke, "let's go talk to him."

"Hang on, we don't want to scare him off," said Jordan. "Let's go in and get food first."

"But what if he leaves?" said Luke.

"Tell you what," I said, "why don't *you* keep an eye on Reeve while we go in and get the food?"

Luke shot me one of his disdainful glances, but didn't argue.

In a few minutes, we were back outside with a big pile of chips and some drinks. Reeve and his kid hadn't gone anywhere, and the table next to him – the same one we'd been sitting at yesterday – was free.

Jordan led the way to the empty table. Reeve saw us coming. His hand froze halfway to his mouth.

"Relax," said Jordan, sitting with her back to him, "we're just getting something to eat."

Luke and I sat down, and Jordan motioned at us to start eating.

"While we're here, though," she went on in an undertone, still not looking at Reeve, "I've got a couple of quick questions for you."

Reeve's son rolled his toy car around the table, completely oblivious.

"We were wondering about those metal security doors," said Jordan, when Reeve didn't answer. "You know, the ones with no handles that you need a key card to—"

"Look guys," said Reeve, twisting around, "I'm just trying to spend some time with my son on my afternoon off, all right? I don't want any trouble."

"And we don't want to give you any," said Jordan

calmly, still not looking at him. "But this is important. Now turn around and stop acting so suspicious."

I shovelled chips into my mouth to hide a smirk.

Reeve looked out across the street, probably making sure we were clear of any other security.

"I don't know what those doors are for," he said. "That's all top-level stuff."

"Could you find out for us?" asked Luke. "That information has to be somewhere, right?"

"I already told you kids, I can't get involved. I've got my family to think about. And you guys shouldn't get caught up in all this either."

"You really think it's that simple?" I said. "We're *all* caught up in it, whether we like it or not. If you knew what was really going on in this place—"

"I know enough to know it's way over my head," said Reeve. "And even if I wanted to help you, there's no way I could get my hands on that kind of info. That stuff's stored in Aaron Ketterley's office."

"Where's that?" said Jordan.

"In his house," said Reeve, "*behind* one of those metal doors."

"Let's say the door wasn't a problem," said Jordan.

"I mean, theoretically. Then what?"

"You'd have the security on the house to deal with, and Ketterley himself, and even if you *did* get in—" He stopped short, shaking his head again. "Listen, I can't do this. I'm sorry. Just let it go, all right?"

"Officer Reeve, please," said Jordan, "there must be *something* you can tell us."

Reeve ignored her and stood up to leave. "Come on, mate," he said, bending down and letting his son climb up onto his back, "let's go to the park."

"You think you're the only one with a family to think about?" Luke called after him.

But Reeve didn't want to hear it. He emptied his tray into the bin and walked away without looking back.

Chapter 17

"Bloody Ranga," I muttered under my breath.

"What was that, Peter?" snapped Mr Hanger, peering down from his desk.

"Nothing, sir."

I was stooped over an upturned desk, scraping at the wads of chewed-up gum with a completely useless metal spatula thing. He'd finally got me into detention after cornering me at the lockers at lunch.

I heard running footsteps in the hallway, and looked up to see Tank come bursting into the room. He'd got a detention this morning for running in the playground. There wasn't actually a rule against running in the playground, but Ranga wasn't about to let that stop him.

"You're late," he snarled.

"Sorry, sir!" Tank panted. "I was … doing something."

Tank is a master of deception.

"Get to work," said Ranga, handing him a butter knife.

Tank flipped over the table next to mine and sat down.

"What are you doing here?" I whispered.

He dug his knife into a blob of gum. "What does it look like?"

"No, I mean since when do you show up to detention?" I said.

"Mike made me come," said Tank, not looking happy about it.

"Huh?"

"Didn't want Ranga to catch me and make me stay back after school," said Tank. He pulled the knife back up, dragging a long stretch of gum out with it. "We've got somewhere to be."

"Course you do," I said.

But then it occurred to me that I'd never straight-out asked Tank where he and the others kept disappearing to. Not without Cat or Mike around, and those two were the brains of the operation. They were both smart enough to know when to keep their mouths shut.

Tank, on the other hand…

"Where are you going, anyway?" I asked, pretending to focus on gum-scraping as Ranga looked down from his desk again.

"Can't tell you," said Tank, scratching his arm through the sleeve of his shirt.

"Why not?"

"Because they told us not to."

"Who?" I asked. "Mike and Cat?"

"No-one," said Tank. "Just shut up about it."

"Come on, mate, I won't tell anyone you—"

"I said shut up, all right?" Tank said, not bothering to keep his voice down. "Just leave it. It's not my fault you didn't get chosen."

"You will *both* get chosen to go and explain yourselves to Mrs Stapleton if those tables aren't spotless by the end of lunch," snapped Mr Ranga, standing up to glare at us.

173

"Sorry, sir," said Tank.

Chosen...

What was that supposed to mean?

Who in their right mind would choose Tank for anything?

I jammed the spatula down into another wad of gum, trying to lever it off the desk, but all I did was smear it out some more.

"Like you care anyway," Tank whispered after a few minutes. "You're just cut because Cat doesn't want you anymore."

I didn't answer. Crap like that wasn't even worth responding to.

Unfortunately, Tank seemed to take that as a sign he was right. He grinned to himself and went back to stabbing gum.

"And anyway," he grunted after another silence. "It's not like *you* don't have secrets."

"Whatever," I said.

"You think I'm stupid?" said Tank. "You think we don't know about all the crap you guys are getting into? Hunter gets here and all of a sudden you guys are *security risks?* What's that about?"

"Don't know what you're talking about, mate."

"Oh yeah?" said Tank. "Then why is there a security officer down there checking out your bike?"

"What?"

"Yeah," Tank smiled at the surprise on my face, "the broken-arm guy. Saw him on the way here. Probably confiscating it or something. Sucks to be you, mate."

I didn't hear a word he said after that.

As soon as the bell rang, I got up, chucked my spatula at Mr Ranga, and ran out of the room. I pushed downstairs, fighting against the tide of kids coming up to their classes.

I ran into Jordan and Luke halfway down.

"Hey, where are you—?"

I raced past without answering. They doubled back and followed me out into the playground, down to the rack where I'd left my bike this morning.

The bike was still there, and it didn't *look* like Reeve had done anything to it.

"What are you doing?" asked Jordan.

"Not sure," I said, bending down to check the tyres.

Nothing. Maybe Tank was just messing with me.

Why would Reeve be stuffing around with my bike, anyway?

"Peter," said Luke, glancing back at the almost-empty playground, "if Pryor sees us out here…"

"Go to class, then," I said. "No-one told you to—"

But then I found it.

A scrap of paper, wedged up under the seat. I stood back up, flattened the page out and read it.

Ketterley @ S. Building 4.30 P.M. Sat.
Security upgrades being put on his house.
Surveillance down for 20 MINS.
Good luck.

Chapter 18

Ketterley's place was on the edge of town, in the block behind the Shackleton Building. I'd been over there for dinner a couple of times, back in the early days, but I couldn't remember ever seeing a giant metal door.

Ketterley lived a few blocks down from Jordan, and his house pushed up against the bushland like hers did. We planned to use that bushland to our advantage: meet at 4.15 p.m. and hide out in bushes until the tech people arrived to upgrade the security on Ketterley's house. Then we'd figure out our odds on actually getting inside.

I decided to show up at 4 p.m.

I'd be the first one there – and maybe Jordan would be the second.

I had news for her. It took an almost sleepless night (which probably would've been almost sleepless anyway, given the latest round of suicidal madness we had planned for today), but I'd finally removed the call restrictions on Pryor's phone. Now we could call anyone we wanted.

If we had reception. Which we didn't.

Progress, though, I told myself as I clambered through the bush, moving parallel to Ketterley's street. *She'll be happy with progress.*

But when I came up on the place where we'd agreed to meet, I saw Jordan and Luke both already there waiting.

And they looked pretty bloody settled too.

They were sitting side by side on a fallen tree, chatting away. Luke was gesturing with his hands like a freaking caveman.

I crept closer, trying to hear what he was saying to her, but then he heard me coming and looked up. I glared at him, and he twisted his face into what he clearly thought was an innocent expression.

"Oh, hey," said Jordan, looking up too. Her eyes were red, face streaked with tears.

I felt fingernails digging into my palms and realized I was clenching my fists. I took a step towards Luke, more than ready to streak *his* face with tears, then caught myself.

Not now. Look after Jordan first.

"Hey," I said. "You OK?"

"Yeah," said Jordan. She rubbed her eyes and stood up. "All good."

"What happened?" I asked.

"Nothing." Jordan peered out at Ketterley's house. "Don't worry. I don't want to talk about it."

You seemed happy enough to talk to him *about it.* What was *he* going to do? He didn't even know her.

I didn't say any of this out loud, though. I didn't say anything.

I just went over and stood next to Jordan, close enough that my arm brushed up against hers. She stepped away, pushing a couple of branches aside for a better look at the house.

Bloody Luke. He was probably the one who'd

convinced her not to talk to me. Trying to squeeze me out. Push her away from me.

And now here we all were, stupidly early, with nothing to do until the tech guys showed up.

I leant back against a tree and settled in for an action-packed half-hour of house-watching. Highlights included a bike going past and Ketterley's next-door neighbour coming out to put something in his rubbish bin.

It felt so ridiculous to be hiding in the bushes, afraid of being spotted. But these were our lives now. It wasn't just security on our backs anymore. It was the whole town. If any one of them spotted us doing something even vaguely suspicious, Calvin would be on us in a shot.

Finally, two guys in light-blue tech uniforms appeared from around the corner. One of them was Malcolm, Tank's dad, every bit as big and sweaty and hairy as his son. He was lugging along a trolley thing filled with equipment. The other one – a new guy I didn't recognize – was struggling along with a massive ladder.

The new guy propped his ladder up against the side

of Ketterley's house and came back to help Mal get the trolley in through the front gate. Then he went up to the front door and let himself inside. Mal grabbed a toolbox and a big reel of electrical cable from the trolley. He stood at the foot of the ladder and waited.

"Why's he just standing there?" asked Luke.

"Probably has to wait for the other guy to turn off the old security before they can start putting the new stuff in," said Jordan.

She was right. A minute later, the new guy came back outside and gave a thumbs-up to Mal, who hoisted the reel of cable over his shoulder and started climbing up onto the roof. New Guy grabbed some stuff from the trolley and headed back inside.

I saw Jordan following Mal with her eyes, tongue poking at the corner of her lip like it always does when she's concentrating. Mal opened his toolbox, squatted down on the roof, showing just a little bit more of himself than we all needed to see, and got to work.

"Let's go," said Jordan, stepping away from her tree.

"Wait," I said, "what about the guy inside?"

"Just don't let him see you," said Jordan.

"Oh, right," I said, following her out onto the street, "hang on a sec while I switch on my invisibility."

We crossed the bike track and bolted up Ketterley's front path.

Mal on the roof. This was not a good thing.

Not that he was *dangerous*. He just hated me. He and I had kind of gotten off on the wrong foot after I accidentally rode his bike into the fountain the week after we all got here. I knew he'd love an excuse to report me to security and this would be the perfect—

A shout from above us.

My eyes shot to the roof, expecting to see Mal staring back down at me. But he must've just smashed his thumb with a hammer or something, because he was still facing the other way, grumbling to himself.

I breathed.

Graceful as a cat, Jordan leapt silently onto the veranda and paused at the front door.

Luke was like a cat too. Like a blind cat with one leg. He thumped up the steps behind me, almost tripping. Jordan whipped around and shushed us both.

Inside, the house was just like mine. Just like every other house in Phoenix. I was pretty much used to all the houses being identical but for some reason it felt creepy and weird all over again.

We crept up the hallway, keeping an ear out for the other techie.

Jordan froze just short of the lounge room doorway. She peered into the room, then jerked her head straight back out again.

In there? I mouthed, pointing through the door.

Jordan nodded. She bolted across the doorway and kept going down the hall.

I followed behind her, catching a fleeting glimpse of the techie screwing something into the ceiling as I flew past.

Jordan stopped again. She was staring at the door that would've led to a bedroom in her house, or to the spare room in mine.

But in Ketterley's house, the door was cold, gleaming steel.

I heard a creaking sound behind me and jerked my head to look down the hallway. Through the open front door, I could see Mal's ladder leaning against the front of the house.

183

The ladder was moving. A giant work boot dropped onto the top rung. Mal was coming back down.

Jordan saw it too. Her hand shot down to grab the doc's key card from her pocket.

More creaks. The other foot came down. Any second now, he'd be low enough to see us.

Jordan pulled out the doctor's key card, and it dawned on me that we didn't actually know if this would work. After seeing More let himself into Pryor's office, we'd just assumed that all the key cards worked in all the doors.

Now wasn't a good time to be proved wrong.

"Oi, Lucas!" Mal yelled, still coming down. "C'mere a sec!"

"Yeah, coming," the other techie yelled back.

Jordan waved the card in front of the sensor on the doorframe. Nothing.

"Do it again!" Luke hissed.

Mal was two rungs away from us. One rung.

I could hear the other guy striding towards the hall.

Jordan tried again.

With a familiar clunk, the door swung open.

We ran inside. Luke heaved the door closed behind

us, with a crash of metal that I seriously hoped sounded quieter from the outside than it did on the inside. He put his ear up against the door.

"I think we're OK," he whispered after a minute.

I scanned the rest of the room. There was an L-shaped leather lounge at one end, and a giant pile of paperwork at the other that probably had Ketterley's desk buried somewhere underneath it. Between them was a huge empty space, like Ketterley was making room to bring in a pool table or something.

All along the back wall, where the windows would be in a normal Phoenix house, there were bookcases stacked with ring binders and document boxes.

"This floor is the same as in the room in the medical centre," said Jordan.

I looked down at the rough grey tiles.

"Same as Pryor's office too," I said.

"What?" said Jordan. "No it isn't."

"Yeah, it is," I said. "You probably didn't notice them because of that massive rug."

"Should we maybe stop arguing about floor coverings and get on with this?" asked Luke, who was already searching the bookcases.

"Right, sorry," said Jordan. She went to help him, while I crossed to Ketterley's desk to try and dig up his laptop.

I found it sitting under a pile of maintenance papers. Password-protected. But I was ready for that.

At least, I hoped I was.

I reached into my back pocket and pulled out a shiny silver memory stick with J.B. scratched into the side. I'd loaded it up this morning with a couple of not-strictly-legal programs I built to help me get around the security on Ketterley's computer.

I plugged in the memory stick and the software got to work.

"Find anything good?" I asked, walking over to the others.

"Just a bunch of forms and stuff," Luke whispered, closing the folder he was flicking through and sticking it back on the shelf. "You?"

"We'll see in a minute," I said.

I glanced at the door, then down at my watch.

4.43 p.m.

Seven minutes left to find some useful information and get out of here.

Assuming Reeve's information had even been reliable in the first place.

I went back around to his laptop. The desktop glowed up at me, a photo of Ketterley and some woman, hidden behind a mess of icons.

I was in.

I clicked through to Ketterley's documents folder and scanned the list for something useful. But unfortunately, there was no folder called TOP-SECRET METAL DOOR INFO.

Ketterley's computer was about as tidy as his desk. Didn't like my chances of finding anything in this mess. I'd just have to drag as much stuff onto the memory stick as I could and sift through it all when I got home.

I hit *select all* and started copying.

"All right," I said, going back to join the others, "couple of minutes and we should be…"

I trailed off. For a second, I thought I'd heard a muffled voice coming from somewhere inside the office. "Did you hear that?" I whispered.

"Hear what?" asked Luke.

"Shh!" I said, walking out into the middle of the room, straining to hear.

There it was again. A voice, or maybe two voices, and footsteps.

I bent down. It almost sounded like they were coming from—

There was a hiss of compressed air and the floor under my feet started moving. I stumbled back, almost tripping.

What?

A square section of tiles, maybe a metre across, was slowly sinking into the ground.

"Out!" I whispered. "Get out!"

But instead of running for the door, Luke panicked and dived behind the lounge.

"Luke!" I hissed. "We need to get—"

Too late. Jordan had just crouched down beside him. And whatever was happening with the floor, it was happening *now*.

I ducked down next to Jordan and twisted around to look under the lounge. The square of tiles had dropped about five centimetres into the floor and was sliding aside to reveal a kind of chute.

"... should be completed by Tuesday," said a no-longer-muffled voice from inside the chute.

It was Ketterley. I heard the sound of footsteps on

metal and a second later, he walked up into the office.

"Good," said another, deeper voice.

More footsteps, and this time they were accompanied by the *clank – clank – clank* of a crutch beating down on the metal steps. Officer Calvin hobbled up behind Ketterley.

And, suddenly, I realized I'd probably just got us all killed.

Ketterley's laptop.

It was still sitting open on his desk.

And my memory stick was still inside.

Chapter 19

**Saturday 30 May
75 days**

Officer Calvin stepped out of the tunnel.

I wedged myself down further into the gap between the lounge and the wall. Nowhere near enough room for all three of us here. I was pressed right up against Jordan, which usually I'd be all for, but right now all my focus was on making sure my breathing didn't sound like Darth Vader.

With another burst of compressed air, the missing tiles slid back into place, hiding the hole in the floor.

"And you're certain this is going to work," Calvin pressed Ketterley. "You're certain this new facility of Weir's is going to be strong enough to contain him."

"Nothing certain about it," said Ketterley. "It *should* hold him, based what the doctor's been able to figure out so far, but we won't know until we get him in there and turn it on."

Ketterley's feet stepped closer. I flattened myself down against the floor. There was a squeak of leather as Ketterley sat down on the lounge. Inches away from us. I could've reached up and smacked him in the back of the head.

"Anyway," he continued, "it's now or never, isn't it? Rob says he'll be dead within the week if he doesn't stop pumping so many sedatives into him."

"Let him die," Calvin grumbled, swaying on his crutch a bit. "We should've killed him as soon as he arrived."

Through the gap under the lounge, I saw him step out with his good leg, pacing across the room.

Headed straight for Ketterley's desk.

"Good luck convincing Noah," said Ketterley, shifting on the lounge. "He's a candidate, however he got here. And the doc's right – if his abilities *are* a side-effect of the fallout, then we need to know about it before we wind up with a whole town full of Crazy Bills to deal with."

Crazy Bill.

That was Dad's secret project. They had him working on a way to keep Bill contained.

"Please don't tell me you believe that," said Calvin. His feet stopped at the desk.

I craned my neck but I couldn't see what he was doing.

"You got a better explanation?" asked Ketterley.

Calvin didn't answer.

"Look Bruce, I know you want him gone. And fair enough after what he did to you. But you gotta be patient. Just let the doctor run his tests and then you can do whatever you want with him." There was another squeak as Ketterley leant forward and stood up again. "You find the report?"

"Yeah," Calvin grunted, shuffling some papers. "Thanks."

He swivelled on his crutch, turning back towards the square of tiles in the middle of the room.

Then he stopped. I'm pretty sure my heart did too.

He swivelled back. Looking at something on the desk. Looking at the laptop.

I heard a *click* as he leant over and pushed down the monitor.

"You shouldn't leave this open," said Calvin gruffly. "Not with the techs coming in."

"Sorry?" said Ketterley. He paused, looking back at the desk.

I stared at his feet. *No. Please, no.*

"Oh," he said, sounding confused. "Huh. Right you are."

Calvin let go of the desk and started limping back across the room. They were leaving.

I felt a two-second break in the panic as Calvin's smashed foot dragged across the floor in front of me. But then he reached the section of tiles they'd come up through.

And then he kept going.

Limping across to the other side of the room.

They weren't leaving through the hole in the ground. They were leaving through the door.

And they were going to walk right past our hiding place.

I gave Jordan a nudge. She got Luke moving, edging his way around the L-bend in the lounge, out of their line of sight. Way too slow.

There was no way all three of us were going to get around in time.

Ketterley cut across in front of Calvin to open the door. He was right next to us now. All he'd have to do was look down…

I glanced back at the others.

Luke had disappeared around the corner, moving quietly for once in his life. Jordan was following.

Ketterley pulled the door open.

Calvin came hobbling past, painfully slowly, like he knew we were here and was just dragging this out on purpose, crutch thudding against the tiles with every step.

Thump.

The open door was giving us some cover now, but there was still nothing to stop Calvin turning his head slightly to the right and finding me cowering on the floor.

Thump.

Jordan's feet slipped around behind the other side of the couch.

Just me left now. Time to move.

Thump.

But suddenly it was like my body had other plans. Like part of me knew that trying to move any further was only going to attract attention.

I froze. Just sat there, not taking my eyes off Calvin and Ketterley.

Thump.

Calvin was halfway through the door.

My eyes twitched around inside my head, trying to look and not look at the same time.

Thump.

Thump.

Thump.

And finally the old cripple was gone.

Ketterley was still at the door. He threw a glance back out across his office, almost as though he sensed he was being watched. I held my breath, positive we were about to be spotted.

But then he turned again. Walked out of the office.

And pulled the door shut behind him.

I took a moment to call off the impending heart attack, then stuck my head around the corner to give the others the all clear.

"Now what?" I asked.

"Now we get out of here," said Jordan.

"With *them* outside?"

"What's your solution? Stay here and wait for them to come back?"

I didn't answer.

"She's right," said Luke, standing up. "We're no safer in here than we are out there."

"Says the guy who dived behind the couch in the first place," I muttered.

"Both of you shut up," said Jordan, heading for the door. "Get ready to run."

I crept across to Ketterley's desk, half-expecting him or Calvin to pop out again from some other hiding place. I pulled the memory stick out of the computer and dashed back to join the others at the door.

Jordan pulled the door open a crack and peered into the hall. I could hear Ketterley's coffee machine buzzing in the next room.

She stuck a hand in the air behind her and counted down with her fingers.

Three. Two. One.

And then she was out in the hall and we were tearing out after her.

We fled past the lounge room without even looking in, and made a break for the front door. I heard a quick snatch of Mal's mate saying sorry, he hadn't realized Ketterley was still here, and then we were outside and sprinting down the garden path.

We were halfway to the gate when I realized that Mal was back up on the roof. He twisted around, reaching for something in his toolbox, and grunted.

Maybe he saw us, maybe he didn't. We were already through the gate and onto the bike track outside.

We didn't stop running until we were around the corner and halfway down the street.

"You do realize," I panted, "that one of these days, your famous run-blindly-through-the-path-of-danger manoeuvre is going to get us all *killed*."

"Oh, stop complaining," said Jordan. "They didn't even have any guns this time."

"Right," I said, "well, nothing to worry about, then."

"Did you find anything on the laptop?" Luke asked me.

I unclenched my fist from around the memory stick. "Good question," I said. "Why don't we go find out?"

Chapter 20

**Sunday 31 May
74 days**

I tore up the path to Luke's house and hit the doorbell.

He'd found something. And whatever it was, he'd been too excited to type a coherent sentence about it.

After escaping Ketterley's office yesterday afternoon, we'd gone back to my place to start trawling through the stuff on the memory stick.

All 8714 files of it.

Invoices and maintenance request forms and photos of Ketterley and a couple of kids who had to be his grandchildren. Kids he'd left behind on the outside.

The longer we searched, the more convinced I became that there was nothing worth finding.

When the 7 p.m. curfew rolled around, we still hadn't found anything useful.

We split the rest of the files up three ways and agreed to email each other as soon as anything turned up.

And we kept looking. And still nothing.

Until about fifteen minutes ago, when Luke had finally struck gold.

At least, I *thought* that's what his email had said.

guys i fund s/thing! coem ovr here rigt now!1

I punched the bell a few more times and Luke's mum finally answered.

She was tired and angry, but trying not to look it.

"Hey, Ms Hunter," I said. "Is Luke around?"

"He's in his room," she sighed, like this was a strange and frustrating place for him to be.

"Uh, thanks," I said, brushing past her and heading upstairs.

I knocked on Luke's door.

"What?" Luke grumbled from inside.

"Mate, it's me," I said, pushing the door open. Luke was sitting on his bed, staring blankly at the TV.

150 Satellite Channels COMING SOON!

Right.

I walked in and sat down in his desk chair. "Jordan not here yet?"

"On her way," said Luke.

I grabbed the remote from the desk and switched the TV off. "So ... yesterday arvo," I said. "You and her just happened to both get there early, did you?"

Luke shot me an exasperated look. "Do we have to talk about this right now?"

"Is there something to talk about?" I asked, skin prickling.

"I already told you there wasn't."

"So she was crying for no reason, was she?"

Luke opened his mouth to answer, then hesitated. "She's been having ... headaches," he said after a minute.

"Headaches," I repeated.

Was that seriously the best he could come up with? Jordan did *not* go to pieces over a sore head.

"Fine, don't believe me," said Luke. "You know, for someone who took forever to believe all this Tabitha stuff was real, you're pretty quick to jump to conspiracy theories about your own friends."

I was on my feet and charging at him before I even knew it, sick of his lies, sick of him taking what wasn't his.

"You reckon I'm stupid?" I said, grabbing at his shirt. "You think I don't—?"

"Wh – Peter, what is this?" Luke held up his hands to block me.

I stumbled back and hit the carpet.

"Peter, c'mon," he said, getting up, "just settle down for a minute, OK? You're acting like—"

"Screw you, mate!" I grunted, aiming a foot up at his stomach.

He jumped back and grabbed my leg out of the air.

"Should I give you boys a minute?"

Jordan was standing in the doorway. She stared down at me, then up at Luke.

He dropped my foot and sat back on the bed, glaring at me like *I* was the unreasonable one.

"Hi," I said, getting up and straightening my shirt.

"Yeah, hi," she said, like she didn't know whether to laugh or give us both a time out. She turned to Luke and said, "Your mum's in a great mood. I take it you talked to her about Montag?"

"He was *here* last night," Luke spat. "I got back from Peter's and found him talking to Mum on the doorstep."

"What did she say?" Jordan asked, sitting down on the end of the bed.

"She tried to deny it all," said Luke. "She told me Montag was here for 'work reasons'. I asked her if sucking his face off outside the medical centre was for work reasons as well, and she went off at me for not respecting her privacy."

"Because she was being *so* private about it," said Jordan.

Luke shrugged. "So, yeah, we're not talking a whole lot at the moment."

Jordan frowned.

Right. Of course. *Instant* sympathy for all of *Luke's* problems.

"So do you want to show us what you found?" I asked, wanting to see it and get out of here.

"Right," said Luke, getting up, apparently putting the fight behind him. Easy enough when you're the one getting everything you want.

He opened his laptop and the screen flashed on.

"I can't believe it took me so long to find this," he said, clicking through a bunch of folders until he got to a slide show file labelled *Network Schematic*, last modified sometime last year.

The first slide was a map of Phoenix.

"That's the map they gave us all when we got here," said Jordan. "The one that came in the welcome pack."

"Yeah," said Luke. "Well, here's what they *don't* show you in the welcome pack…"

He clicked to the next slide. A bunch of grey boxes appeared on the map. Rooms. One in every major building in town.

"That's Pryor's office," I said, pointing to one of the boxes.

"Right," said Luke, tapping the screen. "Pryor's office, Ketterley's office, that room in the Shackleton Building…"

"Montag's too," said Jordan. "All the rooms with

the security doors."

"Yeah," said Luke. "And check this out."

He clicked again.

A thin grey line stretched out from each of the boxes, shooting across the map, towards the centre of town. The lines all came together in one place.

The Shackleton Building.

"Tunnels," I said.

"Uh-huh," said Luke. "Look."

The next slide was a computer-generated side-view of the Shackleton Building, with all the different departments and offices labelled.

There was a grey section marked out underneath the building, below ground level. An underground room where all the tunnels met up.

"What do you reckon it's for?" I wondered out loud. "What are they keeping down there that's so—"

"Not down there," said Luke. "Up here."

He pointed to a tunnel leading out of the room. A tunnel that went straight up.

Luke traced along the path of the tunnel with his finger. It rose into the air, up through the middle of the Shackleton Building, and came out at the top floor.

"But we've already been up there," said Jordan.

Luke had a weird look on his face. "No, we haven't."

"Mate, what are you talking about?" I said, exasperated. "Where do you think we were last Sun—?"

And then it clicked.

The top floor of the Shackleton Building that Dad had shown us last weekend was actually not the top floor at all.

There was another floor above it.

A floor you could only reach by coming in through one of those underground tunnels.

"We have to get up there," said Jordan.

"I dunno," I said. "I mean, that's not just your average, run-of-the-mill suicide mission. We get caught up there and we are all *kinds* of dead. Unless we've got a really good reason to—"

"Are you blind?" snapped Luke. "*There's* our reason!"

He stabbed a finger at a room on the top floor.

A room marked *External Communications*.

Chapter 21

Monday 1 June
73 days

Knowing the way into Shackleton's communications centre was one thing. Actually getting in there and using it, and then getting out without being killed, was a different story altogether. Especially with the new security they were putting up around the entrances. Not to mention the whole town watching our every move.

The only way we'd have any chance of warning the outside was with help from someone on the *inside*.

Which is how we found ourselves walking up to the security centre the next day, with a note for Officer Reeve.

"You're *sure* you've got the right number?" asked Luke as we walked between the fountain and the Shackleton Building, weaving our bikes through the after-school traffic. "If someone else finds that note…"

"I looked it up in the directory this morning," said Jordan. "Relax."

"Yep," I said. "Nothing says *relaxation* like sneaking around behind the security centre to—"

"Shh!" said Jordan. A pair of security guards was coming past. They glared at us as they crossed our path, but they kept walking and didn't give us any trouble.

We waited until they were gone and then turned up the street that runs between the security centre and the Shackleton Building.

"Shouldn't we take another way around?" asked Luke, looking back over his shoulder. "Isn't it kind of suspicious for us to be wandering through here?"

"This is the way I come home every day," I said. "The only thing that's suspicious is you jittering around like an idiot."

Not that we actually had to be *doing* anything suspicious to be treated as suspects these days.

The Shackleton Building loomed on our left. For all we knew, everyone in the building could be staring down at us through the one-way glass. I forced myself not to look up until we were around the corner and out of sight.

We stopped at the row of bike racks at the back of the security centre – the place where all the security staff parked while they were at work. Lucky for us, there were no windows back here.

"All right, start looking," I said, starting down the row of bikes. "Number zero-one-eight-nine."

I kept glancing back at the row of houses on the other side of the track. It wasn't even four o'clock yet. Everyone should still be at work.

So why was I so sure we were being watched?

"Over here," whispered Luke after a minute, hand resting on the seat of one of the bikes.

We dashed over. Jordan pulled a scrap of paper from her pocket.

Need to talk – important.
3.30 p.m. Tuesday @ Romeo IX.

209

She checked the number engraved into the frame of Reeve's bike, then wedged the paper under the seat.

"Done," she said.

Romeo IX was a set of coordinates on the town map. R9. It corresponded to a place along one of the riding paths called the Nest. I just hoped Reeve was smart enough to—

"Hey, what are you guys doing?" squeaked an all-too-familiar voice.

It was Freckles, the Year 7 kid. Ghost was with her.

"Going back to my place," I said, jerking a thumb over my shoulder, down the street.

"Then why are you over here?" asked Freckles, coming towards us. "Only security are allowed to park here."

"Is there something we can do for you guys?" asked Jordan, cutting in before I had a chance to respond.

"Actually, there is," said Freckles, putting her hands on her hips. "We want to know why you guys are still staff-student liaison officers when you've been busted stealing and vandalising and stuff." She elbowed Ghost in the ribs.

"Y-yeah," said Ghost.

"Dunno," I said. "I'm sure Pryor *tried* to come up with a worse punishment than dealing with you everyday, but—"

Jordan put a hand on my shoulder. "Peter…"

Freckles sneered at me. "You're not even doing your job properly," she said. "We've been trying to talk to you for ages, but you guys are never in the playground."

"Funny, that," I said, looking up and down the street.

Ghost stared at the concrete, like he really didn't want to get caught up in this.

"Listen," said Jordan, stepping in front of me and looking down at Freckles. "We're sorry we're not around as much as you'd like. We've just been really busy lately. And I know what people are saying about us – that we're petty criminals or whatever – but a lot of that's just a misunderstanding. I mean, you can't always believe everything you hear, right?"

Freckles thought about this for a minute. Then she rolled her eyes. "Whatever," she said.

She took one last suspicious glance at the bike

racks, and then she and Ghost headed back around the side of the security centre.

Tuesday 2 June
72 days

"I didn't say she wasn't annoying," said Jordan the next day. "I said it's probably not smart to bite her head off every time she comes up to us."

Luke opened his mouth to agree, but I cut in before he had the chance.

"Yeah, no, you're right," I said. "Need to be more careful. But no harm done, right? Pryor's still got nothing on us."

"You keep saying that like it actually means something," said Luke.

We were on our way to Pryor's office with my spectacular forgery of our latest waste-of-time assignment. Staples had caught us on the way into school and asked us to come in at break.

Pryor was waiting in the front office when we got there.

"You're late," she said as soon as we were through

212

the door. Her face had the same dark scowl as when she was questioning us about the phone. She'd clearly given up on the whole best-friends-forever bit. She marched us up the hall, snapped at Staples to make sure we weren't interrupted, and then let us into her office.

Jordan glanced up at the security cameras as she walked in.

"Your assignment, please," said Pryor, stretching a hand out across her desk as soon as we'd all sat down.

"Here you go, miss," I said, handing over the pages. "Some of our best work, I reckon."

Pryor snatched the assignment from me and scanned the first page without speaking. Actually reading it this time. Why? Clearly she wasn't interested in the results. So what was her game?

I waited, feet scuffing against the rug on the floor.

All these months, I'd been convinced she was holed up in here doing whatever it is that normal principals do, when really she was prancing around the Shackleton Building, plotting world domination.

Pryor turned to the second page and kept reading. Her lip curled.

No way had she spotted my fake. She was good, but she wasn't *that* good.

Next to me, Jordan was sitting up way too straight, arms folded in front of her. Nervous. Her eyes kept flitting across in my direction.

Don't worry, I thought, smiling back at her, letting her know it was all OK. *Pryor's got no idea—*

Pryor threw the assignment down on her desk. "I am insulted," she spat.

I tried to look puzzled. "Sorry, miss?"

"This is unacceptable," said Pryor. "I want this assignment completed again from scratch."

"Why, miss?" I said. "What's wrong with—?"

"What's *wrong*, Mr Weir, is your attitude. Your blatant disregard for authority and your unwillingness to take seriously the duties that have been assigned to you."

Jordan glared at me, almost as angry as Pryor. Blaming me.

No. This wasn't my fault.

"Miss, no," I said, "that's not—"

"Did you honestly think you could just shrug off this assignment without my knowledge?" Pryor raised her eyebrows, like she was actually expecting an answer. When I didn't give her one, she got to her feet. "There are no secrets in Phoenix, Mr Weir. I would have hoped I'd made that abundantly clear to you three by now."

She went to the door and shouted at Staples to join us.

"I believe our staff-student liaison officers may require some additional supervision as they complete their next assignment," Pryor told Staples. "I would like you to keep an eye on them. Please ensure that they do not leave school property before four-thirty this afternoon."

Staples gave Pryor a look like she was pretty sure this wasn't in her job description, but said, "Of course."

"Four-thirty?" I said, trying to stay calm and polite. "What for, miss? Won't everyone be out of here ages before then?"

"Not the students in the study centre," said Pryor, eyes glinting. "The library doesn't close until four. We wouldn't want to neglect those students in our statistics, would we?"

"No miss," I said. "We definitely wouldn't want that."

Pryor sat back down again. She picked up our assignment and made a show of dropping it into the recycling bin next to her desk.

"I do hope this isn't a *problem* for you, Mr Weir," she said, suddenly smiling again. "You don't have somewhere else to be this afternoon, do you?"

"She knows," Luke whispered. "She knows we're meant to be meeting Reeve today."

"As if she does," I said.

It was 3.25 p.m. And it was raining.

The school was deserted except for Jordan, Luke and me standing out the front, clipboards in hand, waiting to check off the last few losers on their way out of the library.

"Why else would she make us re-do the assignment?" asked Luke.

"Because she could tell the first one was a fake, that's why," said Jordan, water dripping down her braids.

"Whoa, hey," I said. "I didn't get this far at school by not knowing how to fake an assignment. That Year 7 kid must've said something to her."

"And I wonder who could've made her angry enough to do that," said Jordan.

I shivered in the cold, mind racing for a way to redeem myself.

How long had Freckles been watching us before she spoke up? Long enough to see where we'd hidden the note? Or had she just gone to Pryor to have a whinge about us not doing our jobs properly?

Either way, we were screwed unless we could find a way out of here.

I looked back towards the front office. Staples was standing a few metres away, holding an umbrella and a mug of coffee, looking as frustrated as we were to be stuck out here.

"All right," I said. "Let me handle this."

Jordan shot me a sceptical look. I ignored it and started walking over to Staples.

"Hey, miss!" I called. "You look cold."

Staples' eyes narrowed. "Back to work, Peter."

Usually, Mrs Stapleton wasn't a teacher you tried to negotiate with, but I was betting this whole situation had her just irritated enough to hear me out.

"Ah, don't be like that, miss!" I smiled. "Why don't

we get out of your hair and let you get back inside?"

"It's only three-thirty," said Staples. "Ms Pryor wants you out here for another hour."

"Come on, miss," I said. "Stuff Pryor. She's wasting our time."

"*Peter,*" she barked, but only half-heartedly. "I will not have you speaking so disrespectfully about our head teacher. Whatever either of us may think about the task Ms Pryor has given us, the fact remains that *she* is in charge, and this is her decision."

"Yeah," I said, "but what she doesn't know won't hurt her, will it miss?"

For a second, I swear she almost smiled.

"We'll even swing by the library on the way out," I lied. "Count how many kids are in there and put them on our maps. Everybody wins!"

Staples stared at me for a long moment. She took a sip of her coffee and gazed across in the direction of Pryor's office, shivering slightly.

Then she looked back at me and shook her head. "All right," she sighed, like she was agreeing to this against her better judgement. "Go."

"Thanks, miss!" I grinned. "You're the best!"

"If you breathe *one word* of this to anybody, I will see to it personally that you are expelled from Phoenix High."

"Got it," I said, "Have a good afternoon, miss!"

I came back over to join the others, soaking up the disbelieving expression on Jordan's face as she watched Staples walk away across the grass.

"What did you—?"

"Told you I'd handle it," I said, shoving my clipboard into my backpack. "C'mon. Let's go find Reeve."

Chapter 22

**Tuesday 2 June
72 days**

We rode straight to the south end of town, to the place where all the bike paths and walking trails start out into the bush. It was bucketing down by the time we got there. On the plus side, this meant the streets were all but deserted – no sane person would be out here in this. But the pouring rain also meant that we couldn't count on Reeve waiting around for long.

Assuming he'd come out here in the first place.

Assuming he'd even got the message.

Assuming the million other things that could've gone wrong hadn't gone wrong.

Don't think about it.

We shot straight off the concrete path and down one of the dirt riding tracks. My head swam with déjà vu. This was the same path we'd started out from two weeks ago, when we were following Crazy Bill's map out to the wall. This time around, the path was wet and slippery and turning to mud at the edges. The trees pressed in from both sides, and in my head I saw armed security guards hiding behind every one of them, training their weapons on me.

Then again, anyone out here who wanted me dead could just wait for the pneumonia to set in and save themselves the trouble.

Jordan was ahead of me, dark skin and the outline of a singlet showing up through her soaking white shirt.

More rain. More mud. More imaginary guards with imaginary guns.

And then, finally, I spotted the Nest coming up on our left.

Jordan reached it first. She slid to a stop, sending mud splattering back at Luke and me.

"Sorry."

"No worries," I said, wiping the worst of it away

from my face. I jumped off my bike and checked to make sure no-one else was coming along the path. "All right, let's go."

The Nest is this rock formation that's basically one giant boulder with a couple of little boulders sitting on top of it. Looks nothing like a nest, but whatever. Jordan had decided that this would be a safe enough place for us and Reeve to have our little chat.

We lifted up our bikes and started dragging them off the path, into the bush.

I'd been hoping we wouldn't feel the rain so much once we were under the trees but, if anything, it was worse. All the trees did was collect all the little raindrops and dump them down on top of us in massive sheets.

We tracked around to the far side of the Nest, until we found an outcropping that jutted out far enough for us to cower under. Although by this point, it wasn't like we were getting any wetter.

There was no sign of Reeve. Nothing to do but stand there, staring out at the bushland, watching the rain pelt down all around us.

I tried to listen for footsteps, or the sound of someone moving through the trees, but it was impossible to hear anything over this ridiculous downpour.

"How long do we wait?" I asked after a while.

"We wait until he gets here," said Luke firmly.

"What if he's not coming?" I asked.

"He's coming."

I checked my watch. It was almost 4 p.m. "He might have already been and gone," I said.

Jordan made a noise which I reckon was meant to tell me I was being insensitive. Like I wanted to be right about this.

But drowning out here in this rain wasn't going to help anyone.

I stepped away from the outcropping.

"What are you doing?" Jordan snapped.

"Just gonna do a quick circuit round the rock," I said, holding my hands up. "Make sure Reeve isn't waiting around the other side."

I walked off into the bush, feet squishing through the mud and leaves, dragging my right hand along the rock wall.

Thunder cracked above my head.

This was insane. Who would be dumb enough to—?

I swore loudly as a uniformed arm grabbed my shoulder.

I wrenched my body forward, pulling free of the guard's grip, and stumbled to the ground, sprawling on my hands and knees in the mud. My hand came down on a big stick. I grabbed it, lifted it above my head, and brought it around to—

I stopped in mid-swing.

"Whoa. Easy there, mate." Reeve was staring down at me, looking wary.

"Oh," I said. "Hey. How's it going?"

I dropped the stick, and Reeve reached out to pull me to my feet.

Jordan and Luke came running around the rock towards us. They saw Reeve and their faces lit up.

Reeve was soaking wet like the rest of us. He'd wrapped up his broken arm in a plastic bag or something, but it didn't look like that was doing him much good. The whole left side of his body was covered in mud, like he'd taken a dive off his bike on the way here.

"This had better be good," he said.

Jordan started leading him back towards the outcropping. "We got into Ketterley's office," she said. "Thanks heaps for your note."

Reeve ran a hand down over his face. "I should never have given it to you."

"Yeah, you should," said Luke. "We found out what's behind those security doors."

"That doesn't –" said Reeve. "If someone had seen you… Look, kids, I didn't come out here to help you again. I came to tell you that you need to give this up."

"Give what up?" said Luke.

"All of it," said Reeve. "All of this sneaking around. Do you know what would've happened if I hadn't bailed you back in after being outside the wall?"

"We would've been dead," I said as we reached the outcropping. "Yeah, you told us already."

"Right, and that was *before* you were targeted as security risks," said Reeve. "Something like that happens again and you're not going to walk away from it."

"Then we're just gonna have to try really hard not to get caught," said Jordan.

"Jordan, no," Reeve pleaded, a pained look flashing across his face. "Trust me, whatever you're trying to achieve here, it's not worth getting on the wrong side of Mr Shackleton. I'm not going to help you put your lives in danger."

"It's not *our* lives you should be worried about," said Jordan.

"What's that supposed to mean?" asked Reeve.

Jordan dragged her hands through her hair, pushing the glistening braids back out of her face. She turned to Luke and said, "Show him."

Luke pulled out his phone. It wasn't good for much in this place, but it could still play audio files. Before school this morning, we'd loaded it up with the recording Crazy Bill had given us.

Luke hit play and handed the phone to Reeve.

Static crackled out from the speaker, barely audible over the downpour. Reeve's brow crinkled, like he thought we were having him on. But then he heard Shackleton's voice and his eyes went wide.

For the next few minutes, we watched Reeve's expression shift from shock to disbelief to a sort of shaky despair as he listened to Shackleton and Calvin talk about using Tabitha to "cleanse the outside world of the human plague".

We'd listened to the recording a thousand times before. But, for some reason, seeing Reeve hear it for the first time made the whole thing seem brand-new again.

"A hundred days, Bruce," said Shackleton in his too-polite voice as we reached the end of the recording. "That's all. A hundred more days and then this will all be over."

The recording sputtered and died.

Reeve reached for the side of the rock to steady himself. He stared up at the dark grey sky. I could see his mind ticking over, scrambling for some other explanation, some reason to believe that none of it was real.

Trying to do exactly what I'd done.

"Where did you get that?" he asked eventually, handing the phone back to Luke.

"Does it matter?" asked Jordan.

Reeve didn't answer.

"Like we said," Jordan went on when it was clear that Reeve wasn't going to say anything, "we found out what those security doors are guarding. There's a network of tunnels under the town, leading up to a secret part of the Shackleton Building."

Reeve just nodded. I'd expected him to be at least a little bit surprised by this news, but I guess he'd already reached his maximum shock level for the day.

"There's some kind of communications centre up there," Jordan continued. "We need to get inside and call for help. But first we need *your* help to get us past security."

Still no answer from Reeve. He looked completely dazed, and I wondered if what Jordan had said had gone in, or whether he was still reeling from the recording.

Reeve let go of the rock and stepped out into the rain. He paced a bit, like he was considering just walking away from the conversation.

Then he stopped. He closed his eyes and took a deep breath.

"It'll have to be tomorrow," he said.

Luke's face broke into a grin.

"Whoa – what?" I said. "Tomorrow?"

Reeve opened his eyes again. "There are two

separate security grids in Phoenix," he explained. "Grid One covers the mall, the Shackleton Building, and the security centre. You can access it from any computer in Phoenix, so long as you've got the right security clearance. Then there's Grid Two, which – well, we've never really known *what* it was protecting. But I guess this is it, isn't it? These tunnels of yours. And probably the hidden bit of the Shackleton Building, too."

"Can you shut it down?" asked Luke.

"*Should* be able to," said Reeve, sounding not nearly as confident as I would've liked. "But, like I said, tomorrow night's our only shot. You can't access Grid Two remotely like you can Grid One. The only way to get at it is by going down into the security centre basement and shutting it off manually."

"And you can only do that tomorrow?" said Jordan, shivering in the cold.

"That's when I'm on night shift at the security centre," said Reeve. "It's not usually my job, but Lazarro's still out of action and I've been rostered on to cover one of his shifts."

Lazarro. The security guy Crazy Bill had hospitalized out at the airport.

"But the main reason," Reeve continued, "is that the chief isn't around tomorrow night. He's off overseeing some special project of Shackleton's."

"Perfect," said Jordan, like we were arranging to go see a movie. "Tomorrow, then. What time can you have the security disabled?"

Reeve took a breath, eyes turned up to the clouds again like he couldn't believe he'd let himself get dragged into this.

"Probably best to leave it as late as possible," he said. "Wait until everything dies down in town."

"So, what? Midnight?" said Luke.

"All right," said Reeve heavily. "Yeah. All right. Tomorrow, midnight." Then, like he was having second thoughts, he said, "Guys, are you *sure* you want to do this?"

"You kidding?" I said, as thunder cracked the sky again. "A moonlit stroll into the secret hide-out of a pack of mass-murderers? Who wouldn't want in on *that?*"

We gave Reeve a ten-minute head start towards town, then got back on the bike trail, taking the long way home in case anyone was watching.

The path carved a wide arc through the bush, circling around to emerge at the north end of town, just over from Jordan's house. By now the endless rain had turned the whole trail into a winding mud puddle.

I was still jumpy. Still half-expecting gunfire to start ringing out from among the trees.

Tomorrow.

Were we seriously going through with this?

It was too soon. There was no time to plan. No time to figure out—

"Crap!"

A giant tree root had just appeared out of nowhere. I slammed straight into it and suddenly I was airborne.

I wrenched at the brakes, scanning desperately for a place to land.

The bike touched down again, tyres squelching into the mud at the edge of the trail.

But I wasn't sitting on it anymore.

I soared over the handlebars and tumbled into the bush, somersaulting across the mud and leaves until I smacked into the base of an old eucalyptus tree.

"Peter!"

I sat up, eyes refocusing just in time to see Jordan and Luke sliding towards me.

"I'm all right," I said, moving to get to my feet.

But then my hand came down on something cold and smooth. Something metal. I wrapped my fingers around it, pulling it up out of the mud.

"What's that?" asked Jordan, stretching out a hand.

I grabbed on and stood up, not taking my eyes off the container in my other hand. It was square and grey and rusty, with a silver keyhole on the front. An old cashbox or something.

I wiped a hand across the top of the container, clearing away some of the mud, and instantly regretted it.

Because now there was something else gleaming up at me.

A silver word, scratched into the lid of the box.

Tabitha.

Chapter 23

**Tuesday 2 June
72 days**

I threw the box to the ground and backed away.

"Hey, careful!" said Luke, bending down to pick it up again.

"Me?" I said, suddenly short of breath. "You sure you want to be touching that thing?"

"You sure *you* want to be chucking it around like that?" Luke shot back.

Despite everything, Jordan laughed.

"Come on," she said, "you think Shackleton has the *actual* Tabitha sitting out here in a rusty old box?" She tapped the name on the lid. "Look at the writing. It's from Bill."

"Oh, awesome," I said, "totally safe, then."

Then something clicked, and I was reaching for my wallet, reaching for Crazy Bill's key.

Luke put a hand out to take it from me. I snatched the cashbox from his hand and stuck the key in myself. Perfect fit. I gave it a twist and felt the lock *click* open.

I almost dropped the box again.

He *knew.*

It wasn't an accident that I'd found this thing.

Somehow, Crazy Bill had known that I'd come here. That I'd crash into the bush. That my hand would come down on this exact place in the mud.

He'd left the cashbox here on purpose, knowing I'd find it. And he'd hidden the key in my room so I'd be the only one who could open it.

"How?" I said out loud. "How did he know?"

Another image dropped into my head. Jordan, sitting at Flameburger, knowing Reeve was going to be there.

Don't be stupid, I told myself. *That was just a coincidence.*

And so was this. Had to be.

I glanced up from the cashbox and caught Jordan and Luke frowning at each other.

"What?"

"Nothing," said Jordan, looking away from him. "Hurry up and open it."

The lid creaked a bit as I eased it open. I held my breath, hoping we were dealing with Helpful Bill and not Random Violence Bill today.

The rain was finally starting to thin out a bit now, enough that we could hear each other without raising our voices. I stared down into the open cashbox. Inside, floating on a puddle of murky water, was a DVD in a soggy paper slipcase.

Tabitha Trial – Final.

Before I'd even fully registered what I was seeing, Jordan had whipped her laptop out of her bag and flipped it open, while Luke snatched up the DVD and peeled away the paper.

"Wait," I said, flinging the cashbox into the mud again. "Do we … I mean, if this is … do we really want to see this?"

A gruesome slideshow clicked through my mind – caged animals reduced to piles of splattered meat.

"Are you kidding?" said Jordan, stooping over her laptop to shield it from the rain. "Bill left this here for us to find. He wanted us to know what we're dealing with."

"Really?" I said. "Because last time we talked, he seemed a lot more interested saving his own arse than helping us deal with Tabitha."

"Well, either way," said Jordan, "we still need to know, right?"

She took the disk from Luke and slotted it into the side of her laptop. There was a tiny whir, then the screen blacked out and a video started to play.

We were looking down on a tiny, empty, windowless room, kind of like the interrogation rooms in the security centre. The video looked like it had been taken from a surveillance camera on the ceiling.

The door to the room opened. A man and a woman stumbled in. I recognized them right away.

"Hey," said Luke, "aren't they the two people from that stupid 'Welcome to Phoenix' video?"

"Yeah," I said. "They were actually part of the construction team that built this place. They left a couple of weeks after I—"

I broke off, hit with the sickening realisation that, of course, they hadn't left at all.

The man – Craig, I think his name was – started talking to someone outside the door. No audio on the clip, though, so there was no way to tell what he was saying.

A moment later, another man appeared in the doorway.

It was Calvin. Pre-Crazy-Bill Calvin. Uninjured, and at the top of his game.

He was smiling. Never a good sign.

A woman stepped up behind him, tall and thin, with long, dead-straight brown hair.

"Who's that?" asked Jordan.

"That's Dr Galton," I said. "The one who runs the Shackleton Building."

Dr Galton leant past Calvin to speak to the couple in the room. Her face was blank, expressionless.

She backed away again, and Calvin pulled the door shut, sealing the two of them inside.

The woman – Laura or Lara or something – ran across to the door, but there was no handle on it. She hammered at it few times, and then kicked it.

Craig came over and looked straight up at the camera. He shouted up at us, enraged and scared.

And then suddenly, they dropped to the floor.

Jordan let out a little gasp as they started writhing around, like some invisible force was causing them excruciating pain.

Laura curled up into the foetal position, shuddering, clawing at herself like she was trying to pull off her own skin. Craig crawled over to her, dragging himself across the floor.

The screen jolted as Jordan's hands started to shake. I forced myself to keep watching, grateful that there was no sound.

Craig and Laura clung to each other, eyes closed, twisting in agony. Their mouths were torn apart in silent, gut-wrenching screams.

Then suddenly, there was a flash of red and the two of them were gone.

Disappeared.

Nothing left but a pile of tattered clothes.

"Where did they go?" said Luke shakily.

Almost instantly, the camera shifted. It zoomed in closer and started replaying Craig and Laura's last moments in slow motion.

The whole thing was a thousand times worse at this speed. Every twitch and spasm was intensified and dragged out.

I watched, almost gagging, as their skin began splitting apart, peeling away, bubbling up underneath, like their whole bodies were dissolving. They were boiling alive, disintegrating, bodies eating themselves from the inside out.

Jordan snapped the laptop shut. She gave a shuddering gasp, tears streaming down her face.

I leant forward, arms wrapped around my stomach, breathing unsteady.

There was a retching sound behind me. Luke was hunched over, throwing up in the mud.

I slumped down against the nearest tree, sliding to the ground with my head in my hands. I couldn't move. Couldn't think. Couldn't do anything but watch that video replaying itself over and over in my head.

The retching stopped. Jordan had the closed laptop under one arm and was steadying Luke with the other. Touching him again. And I was too far gone to even care.

The rain spattered around us. I watched the droplets drumming onto the cashbox at my feet, streaming down over the barely legible *Tabitha* scraped into the lid.

Luke coughed a couple of times, wiped his mouth on his sleeve and said, "I don't – What could *do* that to a person?"

I leant forward, gathering the strength to get up. "It's – It's got to be some kind of … I don't know. Like a virus or something, right?" I said. "Some kind of biological weapon."

"Whatever it is, that's what's going to happen to everyone on the outside unless we can do something to stop Shackleton," said Jordan.

She watched me getting to my feet, a searching look in her eyes. *Are you with us?*

I straightened up and moved to stand next to her again.

"Yeah," I said slowly. "You're right. So we'll do something. Tomorrow."

"Tomorrow," Jordan repeated, eyes still red with tears.

Luke let go of her. He rubbed his face and took

a deep breath, like he was psyching himself up for something. Then he pulled the laptop out from under Jordan's arm.

"We should watch the rest of it," he said.

My stomach lurched. But he was right. As much as I hated to admit it, he was right. If there was anything else here that could help us, we needed to see it.

Jordan looked as miserable as I felt, but she didn't look away when Luke opened the laptop again.

The image on the screen skipped a few times, then started playing again.

And we watched in silence as the bloodied bodies of those two innocent construction workers writhed and squirmed and chewed themselves into nothingness.

And in the middle of all of that horror, even though there was nothing we could do to change any of it, at least now somebody knew the truth about what had happened to them.

Somehow that felt like it meant something.

The shredded remains of Craig's and Laura's clothes hit the concrete in slow motion.

And then it was over.

The clip faded to black and the DVD whirred to a stop.

And the three of us just stood there silently for a bit.

Silently enough for me to hear the sound of ragged breathing behind us.

Breathing I recognized.

Cat.

She was right behind us, backing off slowly, trying to get away without being seen. Her mouth opened and closed, failing to form words.

How long had she been standing there?

Long enough.

She turned and ran.

I sprinted after her, bashing through the undergrowth, between the trees, sliding in the mud, snatching at the air behind her back.

A shout and a crash rang through the bush behind me. Luke taking a dive. I kept running.

Cat hit the top of a little rise and vaulted over an enormous fallen tree. I leapt after her, glancing back, expecting to find Jordan right there with me. But either we'd got separated or she'd gone back for Luke.

It was just the two of us now.

Cat took a sharp right. Too sharp. Her right foot lost traction on the wet ground and she went slipping backwards.

I reached out and grabbed her with both hands, pulling her to her feet.

She jerked around, dragging herself free. "Y-you … you g-get away from me, you … y-you…" she stammered, her whole body shuddering.

"Cat, no!" I said. "You don't – that had nothing to do with us!"

But she was beyond hearing it. "Get back!" she screamed. "Don't – don't you *dare*—"

She stumbled off into the bush again, and this time I let her go.

Chapter 24

**Wednesday 3 June
71 days**

When we got to school the next day, Cat showed no sign of ever having run into us.

Maybe she convinced herself that she'd imagined the whole thing. It would've been a perfectly understandable reaction. But somehow I didn't think that's what was going on.

She'd caught us out, up to our necks in apocalypse. And I had a feeling we'd be paying for that before long.

The rain had eased up overnight, but it was back with a vengeance by the morning.

Mr Larson took pity on us at lunch, and let

everyone hang out in his room instead of freezing to death in the playground. Jordan, Luke and I sat up the back and made what little plans we could for that night.

We decided Pryor's office was the safest way in, once Reeve took care of the cameras. At least we could be pretty sure there'd be no-one around. We'd meet at the back gate at 11.45 p.m., sneak inside, and then...

Well, the rest was pretty much up for grabs.

To no-one's surprise, the perfect storm didn't keep Pryor from sending us out with our clipboards. I doubted I'd have much trouble convincing Staples to let us off early again, but Jordan and Luke didn't want to take any risks today.

When 4.30 p.m. finally arrived, we went our separate ways.

After following Luke halfway across town to make sure his and Jordan's separate ways really *were* separate, I went home to my room, searching for some way to pass the next seven hours.

For a while, I tried reading to take my mind off things. It always used to help me. But that was back when the things I was taking my mind off didn't liquefy people's insides.

I gave up and turned to video games. Then email. Then ice-cream. Then video games again.

Eventually I gave up altogether and lay on my bed, staring up at the ceiling.

It wasn't the first time I'd faced death since all of this started. But it was the first time I'd actually known going in that that's what I was doing.

If we got caught up there tonight, that would be the end of it. There'd be no weaselling out of trouble. No escaping. No playing dumb or pleading innocence. You don't *accidentally* wander into a place like that.

I skipped dinner.

At about 8 p.m. Dad knocked on the door.

"You all right, Pete?" he said, walking in and seeing me lying on the bed. He was better on his feet now, but still not great.

"Yeah," I said, sitting up. Fear and suspicion and pity all combining into one dull lurch in the pit of my stomach. "Just tired. Think I might be getting a cold or something."

"That's no good," Dad frowned. "Anyway mate,

I'm off to a meeting in town. Could be a late one. Take it easy tonight, all right?"

"Uh-huh. See you."

He was out of the house before I realized the full weight of what he'd just said.

Dad had a meeting tonight.

Calvin was out tonight too, overseeing a "special project".

Whatever was going on with this cage thing of Crazy Bill's, it was happening *tonight*.

I rolled over on the bed and buried my face in the pillow. As if I needed *that* to worry about on top of everything else.

I got up, walked around the room for a bit, went out and said goodnight to Mum, came back in, changed into some dark-coloured clothes, and got into bed.

I lay there in the dark, eyes open, waiting.

A hundred years later, it was time to go.

I got up, walked halfway out the door, then doubled back.

Crouching on the floor, I reached under my bed for where I'd taped Pryor's phone. I ripped it down and stuck the phone into my sock.

Just in case.

I crept down the stairs and out of the house, keeping watch for Mum coming out of the bedroom, or Dad coming in from his meeting.

It was still raining outside. Not as heavy as before, but enough to soak through my clothes.

I took the path along the back streets into school, staying well clear of the Shackleton Building. It was slow going. Even in the middle of the night, there were a dozen security officers patrolling the streets – and no cover anywhere, except the shadows and the tiny picket fences.

When I finally got to school, I thought I was the first one there. But then I saw movement a few metres away. Jordan was sheltering under the awning of the maths block.

"Hey," I whispered, jumping the gate and walking across to join her.

"You ready?" she asked.

I pulled the hood up over my head. "I don't really know how to answer that question."

Jordan smiled.

"Are you?" I asked.

"Yeah," she said. "I mean, too late to turn back now, right?"

Actually, now was feeling like the *perfect* time to turn back. But I figured that probably wasn't the response she was after.

I moved in closer to her, as though I was trying to get further under the shadow of the building.

"Luke said you're still getting those headaches," I said.

A flicker of frustration crossed Jordan's face. She looked at me for a minute, considering. "Not just headaches," she said. "They're – I think they're part of … something else."

"What d'you mean, *something else?*" I said.

Jordan sighed, like I'd said something wrong. "This why I didn't –" She leant back against the wall. "You'll think I'm going nuts."

"Try me," I said.

"*I* think I'm going nuts. Or, I would if this whole thing wasn't already so out there."

A clang of metal made us both jump.

I looked up and saw Luke clambering in over the fence.

Nice timing, idiot.

"That was close," he said. "I was halfway down the stairs when Mum came out to go to the toilet."

"She see you?" Jordan asked.

"Nah, she was still half-asleep," said Luke. "Good thing, too. Imagine if she'd caught me sneaking around the house like this."

He was dressed all in black with a beanie on his head. He looked like a cat burglar from an old movie.

Luke checked the time on his phone. "Five to," he said. "Should we head over?"

"Not yet," said Jordan. "There'll be guards all over the main street. No point getting any closer to them until we have to."

We waited in the shadows until midnight, then for an extra five minutes on top of that, just to make sure we'd given Reeve enough time to do his thing. Then we left our hiding place and crept to the front of the school.

There were still a few lights on in the quad, shining gleaming circles down onto the wet asphalt. We splashed across to the front office and peered in through the glass door.

"Now what?" I asked.

But Jordan was already reaching into her pocket. She took out a sharp, pointed rock as big as her palm and crouched down at the door.

Luke grabbed her arm. "Jordan, they'll hear you!"

"Not if I do it quietly," said Jordan, pulling away from him. She started tapping the rock gently against the wide glass panel at the bottom of the door.

Luke got up and started scanning the quad for any sign of movement. "They're going to know it was us," he said nervously.

"No they won't," I said. "It's not like a window getting broken in a school is anything—"

SMASH!

I whirled around. "What happened to *quietly?*"

"It was taking too long," said Jordan, clearing the spikes of glass away from the edges of the frame.

That was one explanation. Really, I think Jordan just likes to smash stuff.

"C'mon," she said, crawling in through the hole in the door.

Luke followed right behind her. As soon as he was

inside, he ducked across to the other side of the room and peered out at the main street.

"Doesn't look like anyone noticed," he whispered as I crawled inside and stood up.

"See?" said Jordan, brushing the broken glass off her knees. "Nothing to worry about."

We headed down the hall to Pryor's office. I shivered. This place was bad enough during the day. At night, it was a whole new kind of creepy.

"Uh-oh," said Luke, stopping at Pryor's door. A little red light was flashing up from the key card scanner. "Does that mean the security's still on?"

"No, Reeve would've left the doors switched on deliberately," said Jordan. "Otherwise they'd be stuck bolted shut, right?"

I cringed. "If you say so."

She swiped Montag's key card and the door clunked open.

My eyes shot straight to the ceiling. No blinking lights. Reeve had got the cameras off.

"You bloody legend," I whispered, heading inside.

"All right," said Jordan, pushing the door shut and switching on the lights. "Let's get down there."

"Uh-huh," I said. "Any idea how we actually do that?"

She bent down and started rolling back the rug on Pryor's floor. "The entrance has got to be down here somewhere, right?"

"Here," said Luke. He bent down and started tracing his finger along a tiny groove in the floor, between two lines of grey tiles. The groove ran around in a perfect, metre-wide square.

"Trapdoor under the rug," I muttered, "Unbelievable."

Luke pressed his hands on the middle of the square and pushed. Nothing.

"Can't be pressure-activated," I said. "If it was, it'd be popping open every time someone walked across the room. Maybe there's—"

"Jordan!" said Luke, jumping up. "You all right?"

Jordan was leaning against Pryor's desk with both hands, stooped over like she was about to pass out. Like back in the Shackleton Building.

I stumbled over to give her a hand. She shrugged me off, refusing help as usual, and stood up, squinting.

Definitely not just headaches.

"Yeah … I was only…" she said vaguely, turning to gaze at the enormous old tapestry of the Garden of Eden that hung at the back of the room. I looked at it too, wondering where on earth Pryor thought she fit into *that* story.

But then Jordan cut across in front of me, walking around behind Pryor's chair to the right-hand side of the tapestry. She grabbed hold of the bottom corner and pulled it up.

There was a power outlet set into the wall, behind the tapestry. Nothing plugged into it. Jordan reached down and flicked the two white switches.

A hiss of compressed air blasted out from the floor behind us.

The panel of tiles on Pryor's floor was sinking into the ground.

"No way," I said, as Jordan brushed past to look down into the tunnel. "How did you know?"

"I didn't," said Jordan slowly. "I just … saw it."

The chunk of Pryor's floor slid away into a gap the side of the tunnel, revealing a set of shining silver stairs.

"Well," said Jordan, taking the first step down. "Guess this is it."

In a couple of seconds, she'd disappeared into the tunnel.

I took one last look around the room and followed after her.

Chapter 25

The staircase took us down to a tiny, empty room, about half the size of the office above it.

The walls, floor and ceiling were all panelled with the same gleaming metal as the stairs. Harsh, bright lights glared down from the roof. A doorway at the other end led into a long, narrow tunnel.

I looked up, visualizing the town above my head. The tunnel pointed straight at the Shackleton Building.

We started walking, and I suddenly felt completely exposed.

There was nowhere to hide.

Nothing but tunnel and blinding spotlights.

If anyone else was down here, we were dead.

I looked sideways at Jordan, wanting to ask how the crap she'd known that flicking a couple of power switches would get us into this place. But we were already making too much noise. The narrow tunnel amplified the sound of our footsteps a hundred times.

Every ten metres or so, a security camera pointed down from the ceiling. Even though I knew they were switched off, I still felt like I was being watched. I imagined Pryor making this journey every day, sneaking out right under our feet.

We were getting close to the end of the tunnel now, probably walking underneath the school hall.

There was a door at the end. It slid open as we approached, but not like an ordinary automatic door. This thing was about a foot thick. It clattered into the wall, groaning under its own weight.

"Whoa," I breathed.

The room on the other side was way bigger than the one under Pryor's office. It was perfectly circular, with more doors spaced around the walls – the entrances to the other tunnels.

But it was what was *in* the room that really got my attention. It was like stepping into the world's swankiest bomb shelter.

A row of nine neatly made single beds lined the stretch of wall to our right. One each for Shackleton and his mates. Off to the left, there was a little kitchen area set into the wall, and two frosted-glass doors leading off to what I assumed were bathrooms. Rows of shelves jutted out from the wall on the far side of the room, piled high with boxes and cans of food.

The door clanked shut behind us, resealing itself with a dull thud. The noise reminded me of something, but I couldn't think what.

"What do you reckon it's all for?" Luke wondered, walking out across the silver floor.

"Maybe somewhere for them to hide out," said Jordan. "You know, in case everything doesn't go according to plan."

"Or in case everything *does* go according to plan," I said.

I stood in the middle of the room, looking around for the lift that would take us up to the top of the Shackleton Building.

"Hey, check this out," said Jordan.

Behind us, on either side of the door we'd arrived through, there were about thirty flat-screen TVs mounted to the wall in a giant grid. The screens were all blank, and I couldn't see any obvious way of turning them on.

"Part of the security system?" Jordan suggested, peering up at them.

"Probably," I said. "Either that or Shackleton just really likes PlayStation."

"We should keep going," said Luke. He was pointing to a door on the far side of the room, which I now realized was different to all the others.

The lift.

"Definitely," I said. "This place is starting to—"

A deafening, sub-human roar echoed through the room.

It was coming from somewhere outside. Somewhere close.

"Is that…?" Luke began.

"Yeah," said Jordan. "What should we—?"

"Hide!" I said.

"But he might be able to show us where to—"

Another animal growl rang out, cutting Jordan short. Then more noises that might've been gunshots.

"Does it sound like he's in a talking mood?" I shouted. *"Hide!"*

I sprinted across the room. The others followed.

Behind us, a door began clanking open.

I dived under one of the beds, rolling over just in time to see a crazed, scar-faced man come lumbering in through the half-open door.

Crazy Bill.

They'd cleaned him up since the last time we'd seen him, shaved off his hair and beard, and put him in a white hospital gown. But there was no mistaking those disfiguring burns, those rotting teeth, those wild, bloodshot eyes.

Bill limped across the room, tracking bloody footprints across the metal floor. He'd been shot.

Jordan sent me a pained look from the next bed over. I shook my head at her. We couldn't make this our fight.

Crazy Bill stumbled into the aisle between two shelves of food.

A second later, three security guards came sprinting in, guns drawn. It didn't take them long to find the trail of blood Crazy Bill had left on the ground.

And then—

"Don't shoot!"

Dr Montag burst into the room, carrying a giant syringe.

My dad was right behind him.

I gasped so loud that Luke reached over and thumped me.

Thankfully, the security guys were too busy to notice. They crept across to the shelves where Crazy Bill was hiding, their feet passing inches in front of my face.

"Out you come, Bill," said one of the guards, like he was playing hide-and-seek with a three-year-old. "Nowhere to—"

BOOM!

The shelves went flying. As in actually *flying*. They exploded out from Bill's hiding place, wiping out the first security guard and sending the other two ducking for cover.

Another set of shelves came crashing down on top

of us, crushing the foot of the bed I was under. I shrank back just in time to avoid losing my head.

Crazy Bill let out another furious howl.

I twisted around, trying to see what was going on, but my view was blocked by the wreck of the shelf.

One of the guards let out a shout. It lasted only half a second before it was drowned out by a blast of shattering glass. Something heavy had just crashed into the wall of TVs.

"How—? How did—?" I heard my dad stammer from somewhere nearby. "Sir, there was no way I could've known he was capable of—"

BLAM!

My insides twisted again.

Dad let out a shout. But it was panic, not pain.

Someone had opened fire on Crazy Bill.

"No!" the doctor ordered. "Your orders are to—"

"DO IT!" screamed another voice over top of him. "SHOOT HIM!"

Officer Calvin had just joined the party.

I rolled across to the next bed, desperate to see what was going on.

BLAM! BLAM! BLAM! BLAM!

"Bruce, no!" Montag shouted over the gunfire. "Noah wants him alive! Order your men to stand—"

There was a crash and a scream and the firing stopped.

Then a clattering, groaning sound filled the room. One of the doors was opening.

Peering out through a gap in the mess of broken shelves, I was finally able to catch another glimpse of Crazy Bill. He was across the room, pushing against one of the doors, ready to squeeze through as soon as it opened wide enough.

Calvin, Montag, and one of the security guards were closing in on him, but none of them seemed to want to get too close. Dad was hanging back even further, looking terrified.

I couldn't see any sign of the other two guards.

My stomach was doing laps inside me. I watched Dad trying to pull himself together, watched his mouth open and close.

And suddenly, I knew.

He had no idea what was going on here. No idea.

"Find me!" Bill screamed, still pressing against the

door. "Find me under the ground! I have to – we have to go there together!"

And then he was gone. Through the door and up one of the tunnels.

Montag and the guard ran to catch him, with Calvin limping after them on his crutch.

I saw Dad hesitate, stopping at the door and closing his eyes on this nightmare he'd fallen into.

I wanted to call out. I wanted to shout at him to turn around and go home, to get out of there while he still could.

But by the time I opened my mouth, it was too late.

He'd already slipped through the door and run off to join the others.

Chapter 26

We waited under the beds for a few more minutes to make sure they weren't coming back, then pushed our way out from the wreckage.

The room had been completely decimated by Crazy Bill's rampage. It was nothing but a sea of splintered wood and crumpled metal. Turns out a bomb shelter doesn't work quite so well when the bomb goes off *inside* it.

One of the guards – the one who'd tried to call Bill out of hiding – was still lying where the shelves had flattened him, his boots sticking out like a re-enactment of *The Wizard of Oz*.

The other one was lying on the floor in a pile of jagged rubble. Apparently, he was the heavy object that had been thrown into the wall of TVs.

Neither of them was going to be walking out of here in a hurry.

Did these guys have *any* idea what was going on? Or were they just like the rest of us, innocent bystanders suddenly dragged in way over their heads?

Either way, there was nothing we could do for them now.

We weaved our way through the rubble to the lifts. It seemed impossible that we still had work to do tonight. What had our lives come to that something like this was a distraction on our way to the *real* danger?

The lift slid open.

There was a column of three buttons on the panel inside, all unmarked. Luke shrugged and hit them all.

The doors closed and the lift trundled upwards.

"Well," said Luke after a long silence, "at least we know Crazy Bill is keeping Calvin busy."

"Keeping my dad pretty busy too," I said.

Luke shut his mouth.

The lift came to a stop and opened to an empty room that was barely big enough for the three of us to stand in. There was a metal security door on the opposite wall. I realized it was the one that came out near my dad's office.

We all stayed where we were and the lift got moving again.

"He was talking to us," said Luke suddenly.

"Who?" I said.

"Crazy Bill," said Luke. "Shouting about finding him underground. I think maybe he was—"

"Don't be stupid," I said. "He didn't even know we were there."

The doors reopened, and we found ourselves staring into a shadowy room dotted with glowing computer screens.

We were there.

"Doesn't look like anyone's home," said Jordan, stepping out of the lift. We walked out after her and the doors slid shut, plunging us into darkness.

"Someone find the lights," I whispered.

"No," said Luke, creeping forward, "we should probably—"

But at that instant, there was a loud *clunk* and the lights flickered on by themselves.

"Sensor," said Jordan. "Like out at the airport."

"Wouldn't worry about it," I said, before Luke had a chance to start hyperventilating. "Windows are all tinted, remember? They won't be able to tell from the outside."

The room we were in was half the size of the one Crazy Bill had just trashed. It looked like a pretty standard open-plan office. Computers, filing cabinets, desks strewn with notes, and a few doors around the edges, leading off into other, smaller rooms.

"Low ceiling," said Jordan, reaching up to touch it.

"Makes sense if they're trying to hide another floor up here," I said, heading for the nearest window and looking out over the town. We were above the trees. In daylight, I reckoned we were just about high enough to glimpse the wall sealing us off from the outside.

"Uh ... guys?" said Luke.

He was standing over one of the computers, scrolling through a bunch of thumbnails of photos. As I got closer, I realized that they were all headshots. Faces of people in town.

"It's all of us," said Jordan, as Luke moved down the list. "Everyone in Phoenix."

It was some kind of database. Underneath each photo was the person's name and age, and the same three words in green letters:

Genetic suitability confirmed.

"Genetic suitability?" I said. "For *what?*"

Luke stopped at his own photo. It was the same one that had been sent around with the email from Dr Galton. He clicked the photo and a new page came up with a more detailed profile and a stack of links to even more stuff: academic documents, medical records, police history…

"They knew who we were," he murmured.

"Huh?"

"All this information," said Luke, clicking back to the screen with all the photos. "You don't just put something like this together overnight. They *knew* we were going to come here."

"Course they did," I said. "Only reason any of us are here is because the Co-operative offered jobs to our parents."

"Obviously. But why us?" Luke waved a hand at the screen. "Why *these* two thousand people?"

"Probably our *genetic suitability*," said Jordan. "Whatever that's supposed to mean." She turned away from the computer. "We should find that communications centre."

Luke jumped straight up, like he couldn't believe he was wasting time on photos.

We spread out across the room again.

"Just gonna head up the back," I said. "See if any of those little side offices—"

I caught a glimpse of something moving and bit my tongue.

It was coming from one of the offices across the room. Something was sending a flickering red glow out from under the door.

Luke followed my gaze across the room and mouthed, *is there someone in there?*

"No, they would've heard us by now and come out," said Jordan.

Or maybe they're just waiting for us to come to them, I thought, but my feet were already carrying me across to the glowing door. The others followed, a couple of steps behind.

And then I was close enough to make out the sign

on the door. Two words stamped into the wood in neat silver letters.

External Communications.

I felt my breath catch in my throat. I pulled up short, stopping at the end of a narrow aisle between two rows of computers. Jordan leant in close behind me, peering over my shoulder.

"C'mon," she said, giving me a shove. "Get moving."

The touch sent a shiver up my spine. I rolled my shoulders and nodded.

"Yeah," I said. Then, more confidently, "Yeah. We're doing this."

This was it.

Time to end this nightmare.

Time to hand it all over to someone who could actually do something about it.

I closed the gap to the door, shoved it open, and stepped inside.

Chapter 27

**Thursday 4 June
70 days**

The room was tiny.

Nothing inside but a desk, two chairs, and a flat-screen computer monitor with cords running into a hole in the wall. A slowly spinning Shackleton Co-operative logo lit up the screen, which explained the glow I'd seen through the blinds.

There was no keyboard or mouse. I pulled one of the chairs aside and reached across to tap at the monitor. The screensaver flashed off and a message appeared on the screen.

System Ready.

I tapped the monitor again.

Nothing changed.

"What do we do?" Luke asked, reaching for the screen like it would work if *he* touched it.

"We stop asking stupid questions and let me think about it," I muttered. I knocked his hand out of the way and stood up to examine the monitor.

It took me way longer to figure it out than it should have. My mind was still echoing with gunshots and screaming, and Luke's heavy breathing made me want to lean back and smash his head into the wall.

But I got there eventually. There was a dock at the top of the monitor.

I jumped back from the table, head almost smacking Luke in the teeth, and dropped down to the floor, yanking at the leg of my jeans. I stood back up again, phone in hand.

There was tiny *thunk* as I plugged the phone down into the dock.

A long, continuous warbling blasted from the speakers on either side of the monitor, filling up the room.

A dial tone. I barely even recognized it.

The screen flashed again, revealing a telephone keypad.

"Yes!" I grinned. "All right, who do we—?"

But before I could even get the question out, Luke had shoved me aside and was tapping in a number. The dial tone stopped and the speakers bleeped and blooped with each button he pressed.

No need to ask who he was calling.

I jumped as a hand wrapped around my shoulder. Jordan.

Doing what? Thanking me?

Luke hit the last couple of numbers, and the phone began to ring.

Ring.

Stop.

Ring.

Stop.

I counted them off in my head.

Three … Four … Five…

Jordan's hand weighed heavily on my shoulder.

Each ring seemed to last for about a thousand years.

Six … Seven … Eight … N—

There was a click and the ringing stopped.

Silence.

"Hello…?" Luke breathed, leaning right over the screen.

More silence.

And then a warbled, distorted voice.

"Luke?"

The expression that washed across Luke's face was beyond words. For a minute, it was as though the whole carnival of horrors we'd been through tonight had never happened.

"Luke?" the voice said again. "You there, mate?"

"Dad!" Luke croaked. "Yeah. Yeah, I'm here."

"Luke! Are you all right? I've been trying to call you, but—"

"Yeah, me too," said Luke, tears starting to roll. "But it's not – they've cut the phone lines."

"Who has?" asked Luke's dad, concern darkening his voice. "What's going on out there?"

"It's the Shackleton Co-operative. They're—"

"Your mum's company?"

"Yeah," said Luke, threatening to lose it completely, but looking determined to hold it together until the words were out. "I'm in trouble, Dad. We all are. We need your help."

"Anything, mate. Tell me where you are and I'll—"

"I can't. I don't know where we are. Phoenix isn't— We're out in the desert or something. They're holding us prisoner out here."

Silence from the other end. Jordan's fingernails dug into my shoulder.

"Dad, please," said Luke urgently, "I know it sounds crazy, but I swear—"

"No, Luke, I believe you," his dad cut in.

Luke breathed out, shoulders relaxing very slightly.

There was a ragged sigh from the other end of the line. "What about Mum?" his dad asked. "Is she OK?"

Luke hesitated. I could see him ticking the question over.

"Yeah, Mum's fine," he said after a pause. "We're all fine. But Dad, listen, there's more. They've got some kind of – I don't know, like a biological weapon or something. They're going to release it into the—"

The monitor flashed off.

"Dad...?" said Luke.

He tapped at the screen a couple of times. Nothing happened.

"Dad!" Luke hammered at the monitor with both hands. "No, please..."

"My apologies, children," said a voice from behind us. "I'm afraid we're going to have to end the conversation there."

I whipped around.

Standing in the doorway, dressed in his usual suit and tie, was Mr Shackleton.

Chapter 28

**Thursday 4 June
70 days**

Noah Shackleton.

The man behind the freak show. The man who wanted to put seven billion people through the same torturous, flesh-boiling death that we'd watched Craig and Laura suffer on Crazy Bill's DVD. And Calvin was right behind him.

Shackleton stood there, hands folded neatly in front of him, looking completely unfazed by the sight of Luke using his communications equipment.

Smiling.

It wasn't the cold, dangerous smile that Calvin was giving us over Shackleton's shoulder, or the fake, dopey, pasted-on smile that we were always getting from Pryor. This was a polite, genuine, old-man smile. Almost like he was happy to see us. And somehow that was creepier than anything else.

Calvin stepped forward. He drew his gun and levelled it at the three of us.

"No! Please!" I said desperately, holding my hands up in front of me, like that was going to stop a bullet. "Wait! Let's – Let's just—"

"Out," Calvin boomed.

Shackleton stood aside to let us past, stretching a hand out into the main office like he was inviting us in for a cup of tea.

Calvin pointed to a door marked "Conference Room". He marched us inside, grunting along on his crutch, which – I noticed for the first time – he barely seemed to need anymore, never lowering his gun for a second.

The fear was incredible. All consuming.

I tried to dream up an escape, imagined myself whirling around, grabbing Calvin's gun out of his hand, and turning it on him. And then I imagined how that scene would *actually* play out; me on the floor with a bullet in my head.

My feet lurched forward, one after the other, like a lizard's tail that keeps moving even after it's ripped off the body.

Into the conference room. Giant windows overlooking the town. Long wooden meeting table. Nine leather chairs. Computers. Data projector flashing a Co-operative logo onto the wall.

Nothing useful.

There were no two ways about it this time. We were dead.

"Please," said Shackleton, coming in behind us, "take a seat."

We did as we were told, pulling out the closest three chairs and sitting down at the table.

"Sir," said Calvin impatiently, standing right behind me, "can we just get on with this?"

"Now, now," said Shackleton, taking his seat at the head of the table. "Patience, Bruce. We're not in any hurry, are we?"

"No, sir," Calvin said. But he didn't sit down or holster his gun.

Shackleton clasped his hands together on the table and leant towards us.

Jordan was closest to him. I reached over to squeeze her hand under the table. She squeezed back and I thought that even if I was going to die tonight, at least that was something.

"I'm afraid we have a slight problem," said Shackleton. He paused, as though expecting us to respond. When none of us did, he said, "From what I heard of your telephone conversation, it appears that you three have discovered the true nature of the work we're undertaking here in Phoenix."

"Slaughtering billions of people?" Jordan snapped. "That work, you mean?"

"Yes, that," said Shackleton, as though we were discussing the weather. "As you can imagine, this information is not something we can afford to have getting out into the public sphere. Not for a couple of months, in any case."

He leant back in his chair, looking up at the ceiling for a moment as though turning something over in his head.

"Of course, we can quite easily trace the location of the man you were just speaking to," he said, leaning forward again. "So, within a few hours, he will no

281

longer pose a problem to us."

"No!" Luke shouted. "Mr Shackleton, please, you can't!"

"I think you'll find I can," said Shackleton casually. "Which means that the only question remaining is what to do with the three of you."

"Just do it, then," said Jordan. "If you're going to kill us, drop the theatrics and get it over with."

I almost broke her fingers under the table.

"Yes," said Shackleton, nodding slowly, "that is starting to seem like the best way forward, isn't it?"

He sounded so offhand. Like he could've gone either way. Deciding to end our lives with about as much thought as he would put into deciding what to have for lunch.

"You're insane!" I said, rolling back in my chair.

"Easy," said Calvin, stopping the chair with his hand and bringing his weapon around again.

"Do you think so?" said Shackleton. "Your father said the same thing, and he doesn't know the half of what you children have uncovered. Then again, I suppose such accusations are the price one pays for trying to bring about a better world."

Jordan actually laughed. "Seven billion people dead. That's your better world?"

"Oh, I agree, that part is quite regrettable," said Shackleton. "But I'm afraid it's necessary."

"Necessary for *what?*" Jordan shouted. "What could possibly justify that kind of evil?"

Shackleton let the question hang in the air for a minute.

"*Is* it evil?" he asked. "Is it not humanity's prerogative to determine *for itself* what is evil and what is necessary or good?"

"You think *this* is what humanity wants?" spat Jordan.

I put my head down on the table.

This was not the ideal time to be getting into an argument.

"Perhaps not yet," Shackleton conceded. "However, in seventy days, there will be a *new* humanity. And it is my hope that they will see things quite differently."

"Sir," said Calvin, finally running out of patience, "enough of this. Let me take care of them."

My head snapped back up again.

Shackleton glanced at Calvin, brow creasing in frustration. He was enjoying the conversation and clearly didn't appreciate being interrupted.

But eventually, he breathed another sigh and stood up from the table.

"Yes, very well," he said. "But do it over in the corner. You know what a nightmare it is getting stains out of these chairs."

Calvin grabbed hold of my seat again and spun it around. "On your feet."

"Officer Calvin, please—"

"Do it!" he ordered.

I stood up. The others got up too.

Calvin herded us into the corner of the room.

"Please," I stammered again, falling back against the wall. "No, no, please. Don't do this. Please don't do this."

My fingers clawed the glass behind me, and suddenly it was like someone had flipped a switch in my brain, like all the terror I'd felt so far had just been the warm-up. Nausea flooded my body and I doubled over.

I could feel Luke shaking next to me, cowering.

Not Jordan. Even now, she was refusing to drop eye contact with Calvin.

"The girl first," said Shackleton easily. "Let's be gentlemen about this."

No.

Adrenaline exploded through me and a second later I was standing in front of her, blocking Calvin's path.

"Peter!"

Whump!

Calvin slammed me back into the glass wall, pinning me by the throat with his messed-up arm. His good hand swung around, pointing his gun at Jordan's head.

I squeezed my eyes shut again, grinding my teeth, struggling against the weight of his body and the weight of the rage and terror swirling through me. I heard the click of Calvin's weapon, heard one final thump of his crutch as he braced himself against me, ready to fire.

Don't do this.

Don't do this.

Please—

Chapter 29

"Bruce, wait! Don't!"

BLAM!

Screams. I think one of them was mine.

An angry shout from Calvin.

And then the thump of a body hitting the ground.

I pried my eyes open, scanning the room, brain processing everything at quarter speed.

Jordan still standing.

Luke slumped down next to me, shaking.

No blood.

We were all still here.

Wait. No. Where was Calvin?

Movement on the ground a few metres away.

Somehow, Calvin had wound up flat on his back at the other end of the room.

How…?

Someone had shouted.

Dr Montag.

He was standing outside the doorway, looking frantic.

For one crazy second, I thought he'd taken a shot at Calvin.

But no, the doctor was unarmed.

And unfortunately, it looked like Calvin was fine. He was batting his arms around, reaching for his crutch, confused and disoriented.

The bullet had gone wide, splintering the glass behind Jordan's head.

Shackleton was still standing behind his chair. He glanced back and forth between Calvin, Montag and the three of us, bemused, but still smiling.

And then suddenly, Calvin was stretching out his hand towards us, aiming his weapon at me again.

I scrambled across the carpet, trying to get out of the line of fire.

"Bruce, no!" shouted Montag, stepping between Calvin and us. "We need them."

"Out of the way, doc," growled Calvin, waving his gun at him.

"No, we can't afford—"

"They know about Tabitha!" barked Calvin.

"And this is your plan, is it, Chief?" said Montag. "To destroy every candidate who—"

"Who threatens to expose us? Yes, doc, that's exactly my plan."

"And what exactly do you intend to tell their families?" Montag turned to Shackleton. "Sir, please."

"Yes, yes, all right," said Shackleton, like this was all just an interesting twist in some drama he was watching on TV. "Put the gun down for a moment, will you, Bruce?"

Calvin glared at the doctor, but let his arm drop.

My body gave a kind of shudder. Relief, maybe. By that point my brain was spinning too fast to tell one emotion from another.

"I assume your arrival means the subject has been safely contained?" said Shackleton.

"Yes sir, the chamber seems to be holding," said the

doctor. "But we lost two more men tonight, transferring him. Which, with respect, sir, is all the more reason not to shoot anyone else unless we absolutely—"

"That's not the *real* reason, though, is it, doctor?" Calvin grunted, sitting up.

The doc stiffened. "What are you suggesting?"

Calvin grabbed his crutch and hauled himself to his feet.

"I'm *suggesting*," he sneered, "that we wouldn't even be having this conversation if you hadn't suddenly taken an interest in the Hunter boy's mother. And until you manage to recover your objectivity—"

"Oh, yes," said Montag, "let's have a lesson in objectivity from the man who's just spent half the night trying to exact bloody revenge on—"

"That will do, gentlemen," said Shackleton. He strolled out from behind his chair. "It seems to me," he said, "that a compromise is in order."

By now, Jordan had slid down to the carpet next to Luke and me. I could see her eyes flickering, following Shackleton around the room.

"I'm sure you can see my conundrum," said Shackleton, bending down to talk to us again.

"Whatever his motives may be for wanting to keep you children alive, Dr Montag is correct. We cannot afford to continue haemorrhaging candidates. To lose another three of our number tonight would be disastrous."

He began slowly pacing the length of the table, rubbing his temples like he was the one having a bad night. "However," he continued, "Officer Calvin is *equally* correct in pointing out the foolishness of releasing anyone back into the community who might compromise the success of our operation. What we *need*, therefore, is a way of ensuring that you children keep the information you have uncovered tonight to yourselves."

Shackleton reached the end of the table and stopped pacing. "Go down to my office and fetch the suppressors, will you, doctor?"

For a fraction of a second, Montag hesitated, and I thought he might be about to question Shackleton. But then he just nodded and left the room.

Suppressors?

Jordan looked at me for an explanation. I had nothing for her.

But if even the doctor thought this was a bad idea…

Shackleton came padding back towards our end of the room. "I had hoped, Peter, that your father would be a bit more co-operative after the unpleasantness of our last meeting."

I looked up. He was standing right over me.

"What? No, Mr Shackleton, my dad didn't—"

Shackleton smiled and held up a hand. "I'm not suggesting that he was involved in tonight's little endeavour," he said. "Your father has no idea what goes on up here. However – ah."

The doctor was back, carrying a steel briefcase. He laid the case down on the table and clicked it open.

"They'll need to stand up," said Montag.

Calvin stomped over and kicked me with his good leg. "You heard him."

We got to our feet and he marched us back over to the table.

"Lean over," said the doctor.

"What are you doing to us?" Jordan demanded.

"Please," said Montag. "Just lean forward across the table."

"Doc, no, c'mon," I stammered, "you don't really want to hurt us, do you? This isn't—"

Calvin slammed a hand into my back, knocking me down on the desk. I looked pleadingly at the doc but he refused to make eye contact. He had a kind of faraway look in his eyes, like he was trying to detach himself from the whole situation.

Montag reached into the suitcase and lifted up a shining silver instrument. Like a handgun with a syringe in place of the barrel. I squirmed, nausea rising again, but any thought of escape was wiped out by the sight of Calvin's weapon hovering in the corner of my eye.

"This technology has been a pet project of Dr Galton's for quite some time," said Shackleton, as Montag loaded something into the back of the syringe/gun. "She was so pleased to finally get it up and running."

Montag closed the briefcase and brought the thing around behind me. I flinched, almost throwing up, as he pulled up my shirt and rested a hand on my back.

"Your father was the first to undergo the procedure,"

Shackleton told me, like this was just an interesting piece of trivia. "It was intended to serve as warning."

I felt Montag point the syringe at the small of my back. The cold steel tip sent a shiver up my spine.

Clink.

Montag pulled the trigger and whatever else I was going to say was caught up in an agonised scream. Pain exploded from where the needle hit, sparking up my spine and down my legs, sending me crashing down to the floor.

"A warning," said Shackleton, peering down at me, "about the importance of keeping his son in line. A duty which, I am sad to say, he has clearly failed to live up to."

The doctor moved across to Jordan.

"No," I mumbled, still writhing on the ground. "No, please…"

I wanted to get up, wanted to save her.

But I couldn't—

Clink.

Jordan cried out, and the sound was almost worse than getting hit with the needle. She tried to stay standing, tried to keep looking Shackleton in the eye, but lasted only a few seconds before her legs gave out and she collapsed next to me.

I clutched her arm.

Seconds later, another shout and Luke hit the carpet too.

The three men stood over us. Shackleton, frowning sympathetically. Calvin, completely cold, probably disappointed that we were all still breathing. Montag, looking like his medical detachment was pretty hard to keep up with the three of us thrashing and groaning at his feet.

Slowly, the sharp stabbing pain began to give way to a dull ache. It still hurt plenty, but at least I had my head back together enough to hear Shackleton when he spoke again.

"The worst of the pain should be over within a few minutes," he said gently. "And your legs should return to full strength within a week – assuming you all behave yourselves."

"What's that supposed to mean?" grunted Jordan, sitting up.

"Each of you has just been implanted with a tracking device," said Shackleton. "From the computer in my office, I will now be able to monitor your locations at all times."

Jordan stared up at him, and I knew she was already calculating, already searching for a way to keep fighting him.

Shackleton seemed to guess what she was thinking.

"Any sign of misbehaviour," he said pointedly, "and the pain comes back. The suppressor will block muscle control in your legs, rendering you unable to walk."

He paused, giving the words a chance to sink in, his smile stretching so wide that it looked like his face might split apart.

"Which reminds me," said Shackleton, drumming his hands on the table. "Doctor, would you please ensure that we have a wheelchair waiting for Peter's father when he wakes up in the morning? I would hate for his new condition to interfere with—"

"No!" I said, staggering up to my knees. "Mr Shackleton, come on, he hasn't done anything! He told me to stay *away* from all of this!"

Shackleton sighed sadly. "If only you had listened to him."

I crumpled back down to the floor.

What were we thinking, coming up here?

Why *hadn't* I listened to him? Or to Reeve? Or to the voice of sanity in my own head, screaming all along that we'd be killed?

Now my dad was going to wake up paralysed. Luke's dad would be hunted down by Shackleton's men. We were trapped in this place, *trapped in our own bodies*. And for what?

For *what?*

Jordan reached up and latched onto the edge of the table. Slowly and shakily, she pulled herself to her feet, staring defiantly at Shackleton. She leant in, right up close to him.

And she spat in his face.

Calvin was on her in an instant, but Shackleton waved at him to let go.

He pulled out a handkerchief and wiped his cheek.

"No," said Shackleton, folding up the little square of material and sticking it back into his pocket. "No, it's still not quite enough, is it? Not enough to ensure that you won't make some foolish attempt at retaliation."

When his hand came back from his pocket, it was clutching a phone. He slid it open and dialled a number.

"Victoria," said Shackleton brightly, speaking into the phone. "Can you give me the feed from Surveillance Room One please?"

What now? I thought wearily. After everything we'd been through tonight, what more could this psychopath possibly do to us?

Across the room, the Shackleton Co-operative logo on the screen disappeared. A second later, a security camera feed appeared in its place. It was the room from Crazy Bill's DVD. The room where Craig and Laura had died.

I felt Jordan jolt beside me, like she'd been electrocuted. I grabbed one of the chairs and dragged myself to my feet for a better look at the screen. Luke did the same.

On the screen, we could see Reeve kneeling on the floor, his unbroken hand cuffed to the table in the middle of the interrogation room. He was talking to someone outside the frame.

"As you can see," said Shackleton, "Dr Galton

has managed to resolve the security issues that were plaguing us earlier this evening."

"Let him go," hissed Jordan through gritted teeth.

Shackleton ignored her and put the phone back to his ear. "Any time you're ready," he said. He threw a glance over his shoulder, smiling warmly back at us. "Yes, they're watching."

Cold dread stabbed through me.

"Don't you dare!" said Jordan. "Don't you dare use that *thing* on him!"

"Tabitha?" Shackleton chuckled. "No, I'm afraid that would be quite ineffective at this stage. He's a candidate, after all, just like the three of you."

Another figure strode into the interrogation room, long brown hair trailing behind her.

Dr Galton.

"Fortunately," said Shackleton, watching the screen with interest, "we had a few vials of Tabitha's older, less *discerning* predecessors stored away for just such an occasion."

"No," I yelled, rattling the chair in front of me. "No, no, no, Mr Shackleton, please, you don't have to – we won't say anything! We'll keep it to ourselves!"

Officer Reeve's eyes went wide.

Dr Galton turned around, and I saw the enormous syringe in her right hand.

"Mr Shackleton, *please!*" cried Jordan. She stumbled towards him, but Dr Montag dashed across the room and grabbed her from behind. She pushed and kicked and threw her head back, trying to smash him in the face, but the doctor held on tight.

Calvin raised his gun at Luke and me, just waiting for an excuse to use it.

"He has a family!" Jordan screamed. "He has a *kid!*"

And then it was happening. My mind recorded the whole thing in agonising slow motion. The sudden thrust of Dr Galton's arm, plunging the syringe deep into Reeve's thigh. The desperate shout, echoing through the tinny speaker of Shackleton's phone. The confused pause as, for a moment, nothing happened.

And then the shaking.

Reeve started writhing around on the floor.

Legs no longer supporting him.

Arm still strung above his head by the handcuffs.

Shouting like he was on fire.

And then his skin began to tear. Tiny red lines raced their way across Reeve's arms, legs and face, oozing minute droplets of blood.

But he didn't split apart like Craig and Laura.

He didn't disappear.

He just hung there, screaming his head off and shaking and shaking and shaking, until the strength finally left his body and he collapsed to the ground.

Chapter 30

**Thursday 4 June
70 days**

I stood there, slumped against the table, unable to pull my eyes away from the screen. Luke collapsed over the back of his chair.

"There," smiled Shackleton, snapping the phone shut and pocketing it again. "I believe the point is made."

Jordan exploded.

With one last jerk, she wrenched herself free from the doctor and stumbled towards Shackleton.

But Dr Montag dived after her. He grabbed her around the waist and brought her to the ground right at Shackleton's feet.

Shackleton bent down to look her in the eye. Even now, even after everything he'd done to us, he refused to drop the warm, grandfatherly act.

"Jordan, please calm yourself," he said soothingly. "I can see that you're angry, but if you keep behaving like that, someone else is bound to get hurt. Haven't we all been through enough tonight?"

Montag held Jordan there until she stopped struggling, then let her up and brought her over to me and Luke.

"There's a good girl," Shackleton said, straightening up and smoothing out his suit. He looked up at the screen and sighed. "It's a shame, you know. He really was a tremendous asset to the security team."

"How could you?" said Luke, lifting his head. "He was just—"

"Here are the terms of our agreement," said Shackleton. "You forget everything you know about the true purpose of Phoenix. You spend the next seventy days quietly attending to your schoolwork. You do not put one foot out of line. You do not breathe a word of what you know to anybody. Because if you do –" The security camera feed abruptly dropped out from behind Shackleton. "– I'm afraid that, next time, it will be someone you *truly* care about."

Calvin grunted from across the room, clearly still wishing he could just put a bullet in us.

"My goodness," said Shackleton, examining a silver watch on his sleeve. "What a night. I suppose we'd better get you children home to bed. Doctor Montag, would you be so kind as to escort them out? Officer Calvin and I have a phone call to trace."

Luke let out a strangled sob. I gave his shoulder a tug, and he slowly lifted his head.

Dr Montag nodded at Shackleton and took us away, back down to what everybody else thought was the top floor of the Shackleton Building.

We followed Montag down the hallway, past the rows of Shackleton's nature paintings. Nobody spoke. We were alive, but it didn't feel like it. I felt so tired, and cold, and sick. My back ached. My body was running on remote control.

Jordan staggered in the middle of the hallway. She doubled over and started throwing up. In some dark, back corner of my mind, I noticed that she was standing in the exact spot as she had been the day Dad brought us all up here, when she'd had that dizzy spell or whatever it was.

She leant forward, coughing violently, bracing herself against the wall with both hands. I stood beside her, patting her on the back. Dr Montag waited patiently until she was finished.

We took the main lifts down to the ground, and the doc led us out through the front doors. The rain was still coming down outside, splashing noisily into the fountain. The sky was black and empty, not a single star anywhere.

Montag stopped at the bottom of the steps. He paused, as though waiting for us to—

What? Thank him?

Not happening.

He might've saved us from getting shot, but only because he didn't want a pesky murder putting the brakes on his progress with Luke's mum. He'd still stood by and let Reeve get killed. He'd still raced to protect Shackleton when Jordan had gone for him. He'd still put those *things* into us.

"Straight home, children," said the doctor, finally. He turned away and headed across to the medical centre.

"We killed him," whispered Jordan, when Montag was gone.

"Huh?" I said.

"It's our fault," said Jordan. "It's our fault Reeve is dead."

"No," said Luke. "*They* killed him."

"He didn't even want to help us," said Jordan, shaking her head. "He only did it because—"

"He helped us because he found out what was really going on and he wanted to do something about it," said Luke, obviously struggling to keep his voice steady. "And it wasn't for nothing, either. We got the message out. Some of it anyway. My dad—"

"Mate," I said, my brain too fried to consider whether saying this out loud was actually a good idea. "They're tracing the call. If they find your dad…"

"*Peter,*" Jordan snapped, giving me a dark look.

"They won't," said Luke, starting to sound slightly crazy. "They're not going to find him. He'll get away. My dad won't…"

He broke off as a scream rang out in the street.

A dark shape was moving up the street towards

us. At first I thought it was Crazy Bill, but then it lumbered closer and I realized it was—

"Dad!" said Jordan. "Mum! What's—"

Jordan's mum let out a groan. Jordan's dad hurried her forward, supporting her with one arm and carrying a sobbing Georgia in the other.

"Jordan!" he hissed. "What on *earth* are you doing out here?"

Mrs Burke cried out again.

I heard footsteps behind us. Dr Montag had heard the screaming and was running over.

"Doc!" called Jordan's dad, not stopping to wonder why *he* was out here in the middle of the night. "Thank goodness!"

Montag didn't say a word. He was back in doctor mode, crouching down to examine Mrs Burke.

"It's—" Jordan's mum began, but then another spasm wracked her body.

Georgia buried her face in her dad's shoulder.

"It's the baby," said Jordan's dad, grabbing Montag by the arm. "There's something wrong with the baby!"

Read a sneak preview of

MUTATION

The clock is ticking. . .

Chapter 1

**Thursday 11 June
63 days**

My fists clenched in my lap as Shackleton approached the podium, a hint of his sick, grandfatherly smile still pulling at his lips. He stared down at the coffin, clearing his throat with a sound like a dying animal.

I shivered, digging my nails down through the fabric of my skirt. *You already killed him, you filthy parasite. Isn't that enough?*

"Friends," Shackleton began solemnly, his arms casting long shadows out toward us. "Thank you all so much for being here. Officer Reeve was a dear friend of mine, and it is an honour and a privilege to be laying him to rest here this evening."

We were in a clearing in the bush at the north-west corner of town, where the Shackleton Co-operative had set up a makeshift cemetery. They hadn't thought to include one in the original designs for the town. Phoenix was the one place where people *weren't* supposed to die.

There were maybe fifty people at the funeral. Almost half were colleagues of Reeve's from the security centre, neat rows of black uniforms melting together in the shadows of the trees.

Luke, Peter and I had debated all week whether it was even worth showing up, knowing Shackleton would be running the service, knowing it was only ever going to be an insult to Reeve's memory.

But here we were.

"Reeve was a great man," Shackleton said. "A loving husband, a devoted father, and a security officer of the highest calibre."

Luke leant forward in the seat next to mine. He let out a heavy breath and put his head in his hands.

It had been a week since our disastrous trip to the Shackleton Building. A week since Shackleton had ordered Reeve's brutal execution right in front of us.

Two other men had died that night, but neither of them had been given a memorial service. If anyone asked, they'd been "dismissed due to professional misconduct".

But Reeve had family in Phoenix, so his death was harder to explain away. The Co-operative was forced to concoct an elaborate story about a malfunctioning ventilation unit and Reeve getting sliced up by one of the fans.

They'd done a pretty slick job of it too. Blood on the fan blades. Aaron Ketterley coming forward and corroborating the whole thing. All pretty grizzly, though nothing compared to the true horror of that night.

Almost without thinking, I reached behind and traced a finger over the weeping scab on the small of my back, the mark of my failed attempt to take a kitchen knife to Shackleton's tracking device. It was healing up surprisingly fast, given the mess I'd made.

But the suppressor was still there. A little piece of Shackleton buried in my skin, touching me, dirtying my insides. I didn't care what Luke said, I could *feel* it.

Shackleton paused to survey the crowd, and I drew my hand back to my lap.

"To his wife, Katie, and son, Lachlan," he continued, nodding at a seat in the front row, "I offer my deepest condolences. Know that the Shackleton Co-operative stands beside you in your grief."

Lachlan rocked back and forth on his mum's lap, oblivious to Shackleton's words. He was dressed in a little shirt and tie, tears running down his face. He stared around at the rest of us like he was expecting to find his dad waiting for him somewhere in the crowd.

I imagined Georgia sitting there in his place, all dressed up, trying to make sense of all these miserable grown-ups. I thought of Mum, in and out of the medical centre all week, and I imagined what it would be like if anything happened to her, imagined trying to explain to my little sister why one of *our* parents was never—

Tears pricked my eyes, but I fought them back. No way was Shackleton going to see me lose it.

I caught Peter watching me. Probably trying to figure out if he could get away with putting his hand on my knee. I glared at him and he quickly turned his head the other way.

"If there is anything – *anything* – we can do to ease your suffering in this tragic time," said Shackleton, "please do not hesitate to let me know."

Reeve's wife gave a shaky nod.

I gritted my teeth, not knowing how much longer I could just sit here and absorb this. Shackleton tearing this family apart, murdering an innocent man like it was no worse than squashing a bug, and now standing up there getting weary, grateful smiles from the woman he'd made a widow.

Shackleton paused again, gaze suddenly resting on Luke, Peter and me.

My skin crawled. Shackleton's smile stretched the tiniest bit wider.

'More than anything else, I will remember Officer Reeve as a man dedicated to protecting the town he loved, a man who treasured the values that we at the Shackleton Co-operative hold dear.'

I shifted in my chair. I'd known all along that this night would be a travesty, but to use it to turn Reeve into a poster boy for all the evil being committed in this place …

Luke grabbed hold of my arm, warning me to keep it together. I shook him off, but settled back down into my seat.

"My dear friends," Shackleton spread his arms wide again and lifted his voice, gearing up for his big finish. "What better way to honour the memory of this great man than by working together to ensure that Phoenix continues to be the place of safety, security and freedom that Officer Reeve fought so hard to—"

BOOM!

A second later, the old man was face-down on the ground. The sky flashed orange and the bushland behind him erupted into flame.